Comments

"I think he was quite sensitive and fair in his portrayal of Hiram, but I just wish he had given me better fashion advice. How am I supposed to know what people are wearing these days? Hmmpph."

Lucy

"When the Count told me that Mr. Brown was going to do a write-up on our committee, I was skeptical. And indeed, he used a lot of words that I've never heard before, which I thought was very ungentlemanly. On the other hand, he mentioned low-cut bosoms more than once, which was marvelous. Oh, and I wish he hadn't told everyone that I wasn't smart. It's not my fault. I was born that way."

Reginald

[Translated] "I hate him. I hate everything about him. He's a stupid, American, capitalist pig, and even though he correctly stated that I'm an expert on loose women, it doesn't matter. If he comes to my office, he will be crushed."

His Plumpness,
the Cannon Meister,
Kim Jong Un

"He offends my delicate sensibilities. He called us Devil Bugs. Wrong! We are here to help everyone. We love everyone. We serve all whom we meet. And our teeth are not rotten. The gall of the man."

Carbuncle Spew

"How did he know about me? I thought he did a perfectly lovely job, writing about me. He can come to my forest anytime."

The Orchid Queen

"It was good. I'm only seven, so I don't have much to say, except that I'm glad he included chocolate cake. That was really good. And I liked the mango milkshake."

Anhad

"Since I'm British, and of royal blood, I must be circumspect in my praise. I can say that he did a bang-up job in his depiction of how wonderful I am. Of course, everyone already knows that."

King Hedley

Waking Up Dead and Confused Is a Terrible Thing

Also by Peter Falkenberg Brown

The True Love Thing to Do:
An Interactive Workbook on Finding Love and
Preparing for an Enduring Marriage

The Mystical Love of God:
Divine Writing Messages from the God
Who Is Always with Us

Works in Progress:

The Living Compass of Kindness
and Compassionate Love:
Exploring Love, Beauty, and the Mystical Path

The Postmortem Adventures of Edward Wild:
The Girl in the Tavern

Do You Want to Be Free?
Essays on Freedom as the Foundation
of a World of Love and Beauty

Waking Up Dead and Confused Is a Terrible Thing

Stories of Love, Life, Death, and Redemption

Peter Falkenberg Brown

World Community Press
Gray, Maine

Waking Up Dead and Confused Is a Terrible Thing:
Stories of Love, Life, Death, and Redemption
by Peter Falkenberg Brown

© 2020 by Peter Falkenberg Brown

First Paperback Edition

Published in the United States of America
by the World Community Press
worldcommunitypress.com

This book takes advantage of modern, digital, print-on-demand technologies and may, over time, be printed by more than one printer. If you receive a copy that fails to meet our high expectations of quality, please inform us by emailing:

publishers@worldcommunitypress.com

You may reach the author at peterbrown@worldcommunity.com
if you wish to send him your remarks or feedback about this book.

Cover painting:
"Abstract sky painting," by "Will"
Licensed from stock.adobe.com
Cover design by Great Northern Tea

Interior design by the World Community Press

Many interior illustrations by Great Northern Tea,
with others by a variety of artists, and some by
the World Community Press.
See Image Credits for all image sources.

ISBN: 978-0-9635706-3-5

First Publication Date: November 25, 2020
Publication Edit Date: January 10, 2021

I dedicate this book to the Creator of thought and emotion, to the Creator of writing and stories, to the Creator of everything that makes it possible for an author to write and a reader to read.

I dedicate these stories to everyone who asks questions about life and what "lies beyond." Without questions, where would answers be?

Contents

Stories for All

Stories You Can Read
to Your Children

Preface

This book of short stories explores mysticism and spirituality and the inner world of human beings.

And humor, for a life without humor is, well . . . dull!

I love hearing from readers, with feedback about the stories. If you wish to, you may email me at peterbrown@worldcommunity.com.

I hope you enjoy these wee tales of love, life, death, and redemption!

Peter Falkenberg Brown
Gray, Maine

Acknowledgments

Where do stories come from? Why do we write them? For me, it's often a combination of motivations, inspirations, and circumstances of life. Five special individuals have tremendously impacted my life and have inspired more than one story in this volume. They are, of course, my dear wife, Kimmy Sophia, and our four children, Tymon, Grace, Ranin, and Tadin.

I am also very grateful for the cover design and the story illustrations that were drawn by my friend at Great Northern Tea, as well as the story illustrations drawn by Kimmy Sophia. Sources for all of the images are listed in the back under "Image Credits."

And finally, I most certainly could not have written this book without the inspiration, kindness, and compassionate love of God that touches all of us. Thus, as a writer, I can most gratefully say:

"Deus est auctor amoris et decoris."

("God is the author of love and beauty.")

Stories
for All

Waking Up Dead and Confused
Is a Terrible Thing

*H*iram Hazlacker's last living memory was the sight of the Revenue Men coming down the path to his cave. Hiram called it his Whiskey Cave, even though it was just a bunch of rocks that he'd thrown together to hide his still. The woods of Northern Maine didn't have too many caves, so a body had to make do with what was handy.

Revenue Men had been chasing Hiram for just about forever, the same way that they'd been hunting his daddy and his granddaddy. Whiskey was sacred to the Hazlackers, and they were durned sure that they weren't going to give any illegal profits to some pissant Revenue Men.

He remembered staring at the Revenue Men as they clambered over his piles of old car tires filled with cow manure. They were cursing something awful, which made Hiram feel a twinge of pride.

Twinges are risky little devils, especially when they have the gall to send a signal to your left ventricle to take a break for the day. Hiram would have objected to a twinge like that, except for the dolorous state of death that arrived at his Whiskey Cave just moments before the first Revenue Man had shaken the last bit of cow poop from his boot.

Hiram was altogether confused. How he found himself crouched against the back wall of his cave, he didn't know. Why the Revenue Man kicked what looked like Hiram's body, crumpled at the cave entrance, was even more perplexing. That the man wiped his shoe on Hiram's shirt and then turned toward his fellows and shouted, "The old bugger's dead. Looks like a heart attack," was just rude and disrespectful. Even for a Revenue Man who smelled like ant piss.

They left after a while, dragging Hiram's body with them, taking care to let his body get smeared with manure as they climbed over the tires. Hiram watched them go, peering once more from the mouth of his Whiskey Cave. He was not an emotional man, or so he thought, but as he stared at the last retreating bum of the Revenue Men, he was consumed with panic. He stepped forward instinctively, thinking that he would follow them to find out where they were taking his body.

His panic changed to terror as his foot slipped downward into a vast hole. His head and body and other foot soon followed, and he flailed wildly as he plunged into darkness.

Hiram was observant, having spent most of his life looking out for coyotes and Revenue Men. As he fell through the blackness, he noticed that this particular darkness was much denser than your everyday type of dark. It enveloped him, and squeezed against him, and smelled like lilacs.

He had no idea how long he fell, but at one point, he hollered out in vexation, "Hello! Is anybody there?"

There wasn't any answer. Instead, he drifted in and out of sleep, and dreamt little dreams, odd snippets and images from his life, until finally, he woke with what felt like a bump. Or perhaps a thwump. Whatever it was, it sounded like a body falling to the ground. As he shook his head, he realized that it was his body that had dropped smack dab into a field. He hadn't realized that he had closed his eyes in the darkness as he slept, but since he felt grass under his body, he decided that it might be a good idea to open them. He did so, gingerly, one after the other.

He was indeed sitting in a field. He couldn't place it, so he rubbed his eyes, stood up, and cautiously looked around. He was on a small hill overlooking a tidal inlet, with fields and woods behind him. Assuming that he was dead, he did what any reasonable whiskey man would do. He opened his mouth and asked, "Hello? Anyone? Is this hell? I thought there would be flames."

"No, Hiram. This is Portland."

He was so startled that he had received an answer that he clenched his fists and turned in a circle, looking for the person who had spoken. He saw no one and gritted his teeth. "Who's there?"

"You can call me Lucy."

He turned again, scowling. "Where are you? I can't see you."

"I'm right here. By the tree."

Hiram saw only one tree, a few feet away, and there wasn't a single person under it, of that he was sure.

"You're lying. There's no one there."

"You can't see me?"

"No! Tell me where you are!"

"Very strange. Very, very strange."

Hiram stared at the tree, but couldn't see anyone. The woman who stood there frowned, perplexed at Hiram's inability to see her. She was of medium height and build, and was dressed in such an extraordinary mishmash of styles that if Hiram had been able to see her, he would have immediately asked her where she did her shopping.

She stepped over to Hiram and stood in front of him and stared at him. After looking at him intently, she nodded and said, "Oh, I understand. You're confused. That's why you can't see me."

He sensed the direction that her voice came from and lunged forward to grab her, but as his hand approached her body, it was stopped by an undulating, invisible barrier.

Lucy smiled and said, "Sorry, Hiram, you can't touch me either, until you get over your confusion. And even then, you have to be respectful. I am an angel, you know."

"Yeah, right."

"Yes, really," she said. "What else would I be?"

"The devil," he replied. "My mum told me about the devil."

Lucy laughed: a big belly laugh that rose up and seemed to bounce off the sky. Hiram was startled but said nothing since he wasn't sure if she really was the devil. Lucy continued to laugh until she had to lean against the tree for support. Sputtering weakly, she turned back to Hiram with a smile.

"No, silly. If I were the devil, you'd already be in a very nasty place. Someplace icky and chilly and probably muddy. I've told you already; this isn't hell. It's only Portland. Most people like it."

Hiram felt very confused. Talking to an angel was a new experience for him, and, since he couldn't even see who he was talking to, it made him wonder if the whiskey had finally addled his brain.

"No, Hiram, you're not insane."

He jumped back. "You can read my thoughts?"

"Of course. I'm an angel."

"That's not fair!" He walked back and forth and waved toward the river. "So why'd you bring me here? I'm dead, right? What's Portland got to do with it?"

Lucy sat down on the grass next to the tree and smoothed out her skirt. "Don't you remember? You were born in Portland."

"So?"

"Well, we usually start reviews at a person's place of birth."

"Reviews?" He stopped pacing and folded his arms over his chest. "I don't like reviews. What review?"

Lucy smiled and looked at Hiram kindly. "I know you spent a lot of time in your Whiskey Cave, so you might not have heard of life reviews before. You'll get to have one of those a bit later. It's where your life passes before your eyes at super speed, and you see all the things you've done. But this review is a little different."

Hiram looked worried. "What do you mean?"

"Because you're so confused, I've been sent to help you figure out where you belong."

"Belong?" asked Hiram.

"Yes," said Lucy. "You know, in heaven or hell, or somewhere in between." She jumped up and started walking down a path toward the edge of the field. "Follow me, Hiram. We can talk as we walk into town."

"Follow you?" He frowned. "I can't even see you. How do I follow you?"

She turned and smiled. "Just start walking. I'm like a magnet."

Hiram shook his head and sighed. Walking across a field following an invisible angel was not at all what he had expected when he woke up that morning. He had lived alone, in a broken-down shack in the woods, a few hundred yards from his Whiskey Cave. He didn't even have a hound dog or a rooster. Just a coffee pot, for a body couldn't live without a coffee pot and a goodly supply of dark roasted coffee. Drunk black, of course.

He had spent most of his time making whiskey, drinking whiskey, and selling whiskey to the farmers and hunters scattered around his neck of the woods. He was famous for his whiskey, and famous for his furtiveness. Maybe that's why his heart gave out when he saw the Revenue Men. In all of his sixty years of life, he'd always somehow managed to escape the government men and build a new cave deeper into the woods. The Maine woods were vast, and Hiram knew how to hide.

He also never forgot his daddy's dying words, croaked out as the old man wiped the last sip of whiskey from his beard.

"Hiram," whispered the old man. "Hiram, don't you ever forget what I taught you. Game the system, boy, game the system. You're smarter than those government folks, with their ungodly taxes and regulations. Stay one step ahead, boy, and you'll survive to die like me, happy in your cot, sippin' whiskey until the very end."

His daddy's maxim came back to him as he followed Lucy across the fields. Game the system. He could do that. As they stepped out onto a road, he caught up to Lucy, or at least he thought he did, based on her strange magnetic pull. He looked around as they started walking along the shoulder of the road.

"This doesn't look like Portland," he said.

Lucy pointed down the road. "No, Portland's over the bridge. This is Route 1 in Falmouth. I said Portland before, because we're right on the edge, and that's where we're going. I like to greet my charges in a quiet place."

"Oh," replied Hiram. He thought for a few minutes as they walked. Then, with a sly smile, he said, "So, tell me more about this heaven and hell business. How's it all decided?"

"It's simple," said Lucy. "You go to the place that reflects your essence. Your heart, your character, your spirit. If you eat puppies for breakfast, you go to the place where the puppy eaters live. It's not a nice place at all. And there are no puppies."

Hiram looked relieved. "I don't eat puppies! I never eat rats. I don't even eat squirrels. Well, not recently. Not since that red squirrel gave me diarrhea. I think I left it out too long. Now I have black coffee and eggs for breakfast."

Lucy grinned. "Excellent, Hiram. So, where do you think you should go?"

Hiram looked triumphant. This was the opening he'd been waiting for. "I was raised by my mum in the Bible Fire Church of the Saved by Grace Redeemers. I should go to that heaven. I always liked the girls at church, and the music was tolerable."

Lucy nodded. "Okay. Let's ask them. There aren't very many people in that department, so this should be interesting."

"Ask them?"

"Yes, indeed. It's not up to me." Lucy waved her fingers in the air, and suddenly Hiram heard a dial tone, followed by a ring and a man's voice.

"Hello, friend. This is Nathan speaking, and you've reached the Department of Salvation of the Bible Fire Church of the Saved by Grace Redeemers. How may I help you?"

"Hi, Nathan. This is Lucy. I've got Hiram Hazlacker with me. He's inquiring about entrance into your area of the afterlife, and wants to discuss that with you."

Nathan sounded pleased as he said, "Hello, Hiram! I'll try to help."

Hiram looked around, and said, "Lucy, exactly where is Nathan right now? Is he here with you?"

Lucy laughed. "No, sweetie. Didn't you hear the phone ring? He's a long way away, in the area of the spiritual world reserved for the faithful members of the Bible Fire Church of the Saved by Grace Redeemers. I'm not sure exactly where it is or what it's like. I've never been there."

Nathan interjected. "It's a great place, Lucy. We sing all day and pray loudly in between. We're happy, happy, happy. The girls wear long dresses, buttoned up to the neck, and we're so relieved that we no longer feel any enticement to sin. No cigarettes or cigars, no nasty TV shows, and no whiskey or beer. As I said, it's a happy place."

There was the sound of rustling papers. "Let me see," Nathan said. "Hmm. Hiram, I don't see your name on the active rolls. Are you sure it was this church? Anyway, we could fit you in if you sincerely believe on Jesus and want to live a spirit-filled and holy life."

Hiram wasn't sure where Lucy was, but he thought she was on his left, so he waved his hands madly in that direction, mouthing the words, "No, no, no! Hang up!"

Lucy smiled, amused at his frantic motions. "Nathan, thanks for your time. I don't think Hiram will be a good fit."

"Oh," said Nathan. He sighed glumly. "Oh, well. No problem. Hiram, let us know if you change your mind. Jesus loves you."

"Take care, Nathan. Goodbye." Lucy waved her fingers, and the phone clicked.

Turning to Hiram, she said, "My, oh my, Hiram. Was it the buttoned-up necklines, or the singing and praying, or the lack of whiskey?"

Hiram rubbed his head in embarrassment. "All of them."

They walked for a while, down Route 1, past trim little homes with manicured lawns. They soon reached the bridge separating Falmouth from Portland and stopped for a moment to look at the water. Hiram hadn't spent much time near the ocean, preferring the deep woods with their mossy nooks and dark corners. He felt a little naked on the bridge, and shivered, looking around for Revenue Men before he remembered that they couldn't catch him anymore. Unless, of course, they were in hell, waiting for him, grinning at him, sipping whiskey that he couldn't drink.

They continued on their journey, past Back Bay, and then up to the Eastern Promenade, where they stopped for a moment to look down at Casco Bay. They turned back onto Congress Street and walked over the hill toward the downtown area. Hiram hadn't been in Portland for a long time and looked at the buildings with curiosity.

As they passed a cemetery, Hiram stopped and said, "Lucy, wait."

A woman was standing at the cemetery's fence, clutching the bars and staring at the graves sadly. Hiram went up to her and stood next to her. He turned to her and said, "They're not dead, you know. Just look at me. Still kicking, even after I died of a heart attack. Don't be sad, ma'am."

The woman didn't respond and just stared straight ahead. Lucy gazed at Hiram thoughtfully and then said, "Hiram, she can't see you or hear you."

Hiram shook his head sadly. "I figured she might not be able to, but it was worth a shot."

They continued walking until they came upon a Catholic church. Hiram looked at it and snapped his fingers.

"Lucy, I want to go to Catholic heaven."

Lucy raised an eyebrow. "Really? Why is that?"

"I've watched a lot of gangster movies, and it looks like a pretty good deal. The dons go to confession and get absolved, and then go back to their restaurants and eat pasta and shoot people. I didn't shoot anyone, so I should be okay. And I like pasta. But not opera."

Lucy shrugged and said, "Let's check."

As they continued to walk, she moved her fingers in the air, and the invisible phone rang. A voice thick with the accent of sun and olive oil answered.

"Yes, my dearly beloved. This is Padre Antonio. You wish to confess? To offer a prayer? To light a candle? What is it that will make you happy?"

"Hello, Padre. This is Lucy."

"Ah, Lucy. How was your trip to Tahiti? Did you get a chance to swim?"

Lucy looked slightly embarrassed, which, of course, Hiram didn't see. "Wonderful, Padre. And yes, I swam a lot, thank you. I'm in Maine now, with Hiram Hazlacker. He wants to come to Catholic heaven. What are his options?"

"Hello, Hiram, my friend. Was your death painful?"

Hiram thought for a moment and shook his head. "I don't remember. I had a heart attack and fell down a hole, and then I met Lucy."

"Ah, the falling-down-the-hole situation. Yes, I know about that. My condolences on your confusion."

"Thank you. I guess," said Hiram. "So, Padre, I think that Catholic heaven would be good for me. I'm a whiskey man, and I know how much priests like a good glass now and again. I could keep your friends well supplied. And I'm fine with going to confession as often as you want me to. I mean, if the Mafia can do it, then it shouldn't be too hard for me. I'm not that bad."

There was a pause, and Hiram heard a low murmur on the phone. He couldn't make out the words, but it sounded like Padre Antonio was consulting with someone. The murmuring stopped, and the priest cleared his throat.

"Well, Hiram, you certainly passed the test for part two of the sacrament of confession, which is to be willing to confess your sins fully, in kind and in number. Do you agree to that?"

Hiram nodded. "Sure, Padre. I got no problem with that."

Padre Antonio's voice sounded pleased. "Bless you, my son. There are two other parts of the sacrament. The first one is that you must be contrite and sorry for your sins. Are you sorry, my son?"

"Oh, yes, Padre, very sorry."

"Very good. Very good. Then there is part three. You must be willing to do penance and make amends for your sins. Of course, it's also highly advisable to stop sinning; otherwise, you'll be doing a lot of penance, which is often not very enjoyable."

"No problem, Padre. This sounds like a good deal."

"Then let's begin, my son, with your confession. What do you have to confess?"

Hiram opened his mouth and then closed it again. They had arrived at Monument Square, and Hiram availed himself of the monument's base and sat down. He sat and didn't know what to say.

"My son, do you have anything to confess?" The priest's voice was patient.

Hiram shook his head and said, "I can't think of anything, Padre. Sorry about that. I guess Catholic heaven isn't for me."

"Don't worry, my son," the priest replied. "Sincere confession can only come after a certain amount of self-awareness. It is a matter of growth to know oneself. Lucy, do call again, my friend."

"I will," said Lucy. The phone clicked off, and Lucy sat next to Hiram, who looked even more confused than he had been before.

They sat for a while and watched the people walking through the square. Hiram was feeling rather desperate since he didn't want to go to the land of puppy eaters or some other equally dreadful place. He put his head in his hands and almost fell asleep in the midst of his depression.

On a whim, he plucked an idea out of the recesses of his mind and said, "Okay, Lucy, how 'bout this? I heard that those Hindus have all kinds of gods and even have the Kama Sutra. I could probably fit in there, don't you think?"

Lucy was leaning her cheek on her palm, watching him think. She straightened up and smiled and said, "I will make the call."

Her fingers traced a pattern in the air, and a female voice answered. "Good afternoon. This is Saavi, in the Karma Records Department. How may I be of service?"

"Hello, Saavi, this is Lucy. I'm one of the angels working with the deceased. I'm here with a gentleman from Maine, named Hiram Hazlacker. He believes he may be a good candidate for the Hindu heaven."

"Hello, Mr. Hazlacker. This is Saavi. Please hold on while I look up your status."

Hiram stared at Lucy. "Status? What does she mean? What about the Kama Sutra and the palm trees?"

Lucy held up a finger and said, "Let's see."

They heard the sound of typing, and then Saavi said, "How do you spell 'Hazlacker'?"

"H-a-z-l-a-c-k-e-r," replied Lucy.

There was more typing, and then Saavi spoke, in a sympathetic voice. "I am very sorry, Mr. Hazlacker. It shows here that after experiencing a certain amount of uncomfortable situations in the afterlife involving tax officials and audits and prison, you have been assigned to return to earth as a red squirrel. My sincere condolences. But please do remember that red squirrels are very friendly and honorable creatures, and much better than banana slugs."

"Thank you, Saavi," Lucy said. "Shukriya."

"You are very welcome, Miss Lucy. It was my honor to serve you. Good afternoon."

The phone went dead, and Hiram slumped back against the monument in shock. Gaming the system was proving to be complicated.

"A banana slug!" he moaned. "A red squirrel! I hate red squirrels. They give me the runs."

Lucy stood up and waved her fingers in the air and then started speaking. Hiram looked dully in her direction, but couldn't hear the conversation. After a few moments, she smiled and sat down next to Hiram.

"I have good news," she said.

"Yeah? What? I'm going to become a red squirrel in a church choir doing penance?"

"No, my dear. I said I have good news. Come now, sit up straight."

Hiram dragged himself upright and sat, looking at her.

Then he looked again, and again. "Wait! I can see you! What happened?"

"That's part of my lovely news," Lucy replied.

Hiram stared at her, fascinated to finally see her. He hadn't known that angels could be so gorgeous. He looked and looked, and then he said, "That's quite an outfit."

Lucy blushed and looked at her clothes. "I made them myself. I visit so many types of people that I get mixed up sometimes. Do you not like them?"

Hiram smiled. "They're real interesting. And cute, too."

She blushed again and said, "Thank you, Hiram. I'm glad that you can finally see me."

She looked at him with a smile and said, "I have spoken with my superior, and we have clarified your situation."

Hiram looked at her, waiting, not knowing what to say.

Lucy continued. "As you have seen, the spirit world has all kinds of belief systems."

"Yeah, I noticed," he said.

"Well, there are certain common themes, and, as you might say, Hiram, today was your lucky day."

"Because I died?" he asked.

"No, not that," she replied. "Do you remember the woman standing by the cemetery?"

"Yes."

"Do you remember what happened?"

"I spoke to her. So?"

Lucy took his hands in hers. He was surprised by how warm and tingly her hands felt.

"You were kind, Hiram. You didn't need to be kind, but you were."

He was silent for a bit and looked at her hands, avoiding her gaze. He didn't know what to say.

She slid her right hand out of his and lifted his chin and looked at him with a gaze that was warmer than any he had ever seen.

"Life is much simpler than people make out, Hiram. You were kind to a woman who felt grief. That is who you really are. Yes, you've been a Whiskey Man, and you've been gaming the system, and dodging the Revenue Men. But you've also been kind. Kind to your customers and many other people besides."

Hiram's eyes were stinging. He wasn't sure why. He blinked rapidly.

"What does that all mean?" he asked. "Does that mean I don't have to come back as a red squirrel?"

Lucy laughed and clapped her hands. "Of course not! Did you want to come back as a squirrel?"

"No," he replied.

"I wouldn't think so," she said.

She stood up and helped him stand up. Pointing up the street, she said, "Let's walk."

He looked up the street nervously. "Where are we going? Where am I going?"

Lucy linked her arm through his and said, "Somewhere where you can be kind, and somewhere with trees and woods, which you like very much. I'm sorry, though, I don't think there will be any whiskey. And there will be work to do. You have a lot of work to do."

"You mean like breaking rocks in prison?"

She laughed. "No, not that kind of work. Work on your character. Internal work. Learning how to be a better person."

Hiram stared at her. "Oh. But no whiskey?"

She shook her head. "No whiskey, Hiram. But I can guarantee you that you will not be a squirrel."

He looked relieved. "Well, in that case, lead on."

They walked up Congress Street, arm in arm. If passersby had been able to see Hiram, they would have smiled at him.

Not because he was a woodsman from Northern Maine. Not because he was walking with a lovely angel wearing a mishmash wardrobe.

No, they would have smiled because Hiram Hazlacker's face was illuminated with the serenity of a man who was no longer confused.

The sentence "I never eat rats" was used in this story in honor of our daughter, Grace, who, when she was approximately three, announced quite positively, "I never eat rats."

As her parents, we were very happy to hear that.

Vagabond Sleep

Wandering between the wrinkles
    in the sheets
My mind chews
    on the tattered rags of stress.
Vagabond, furtive, recalcitrant;
    Sleep is a prey to be hunted.
Time is unsympathetic,
    Intellectual and yawning,
Ensconced in the smug repose
    of easy victory.
Twisted under rumpled covers,
    a pillow becomes
A battleground; bruised and cratered
    with the aftermath
    of violence.

Mercenaries with advertisements
    of surefire solutions
Shamelessly hawk their wares:
        "Medicines; elixirs; late-night TV."
        All are bunk.
Each night is an adventure
    with waterlogged boots
    and a missing map.
Sleep, however,
        is a tramp with no gumption.
Huddled at a cold fire,
        Weary; slurring his words,
        He confesses defeat,
Tempered by a parting shot
        hurled with consummate brass.
"What took you so long?"

The Ad Hoc Committee
to Save the Queen

It was a mad scheme. The Count knew this, for he was not at all mad. Grim. Formal. Humorless. Boring. But not mad. Even his enemies at court admitted that the Count was a fount of common sense. His only friend, as well as his increasingly-old mother, would sigh in unison as they bit into their crumpets at tea time. They would sigh, and nod, and admit that the Count was too boring to be mad.

It was thus that the Count almost forgot that he was fencing when the idea occurred to him. He was reminded of his whereabouts when his young friend Reginald proudly poked him in the chest, after a very clever triple riposte, sending the Count stumbling backward, dropping his foil on the ground. The Count was chagrined but managed a stiff bow of congratulations before he fled to his chambers.

He refused to answer the door when his mother knocked that night, wondering why he had not come to dinner. The Count shouted at her roughly, embroiled as he was in the darkness of his mood. He was sorry to have been rude, but what was a man to do, when he had decided to murder a Queen?

The Count never did anything lightly. When he dressed, it was with calm deliberation and an absolute rigor of habit that astonished his valet. The right leg must go into one's trousers first. Never the left leg. To do so would be plebeian and sloppy. The Count was never sloppy. Sloppiness was for the twits at court who ogled the bosoms of the Queen's ladies-in-waiting. It was no excuse at all that their necklines were perilously low, and in some cases lower than that. More than once, the Count had seen one of the idiots drool as he stumbled after a member of the fairer sex. The Count did not drool.

Fidelity and devotion to the kingdom were the Count's raison d'être. He had fought in many battles, boldly risking his life for the magnificent old King. He had killed many men, each with a single rapier thrust, each as a service to his country. When the borders were finally secure, he had tended the King in his sickness until the old man had passed away with a hiccup and a very loud burp. It was an undignified thing for a King to do, so the Count had ordered all of those present to never speak of it again.

Then, after years of service, the Count was reduced to the ignominy of waiting upon a Queen who was silly. The old King had cruelly left the world without siring a son. Instead, he had a daughter, a young snip of a foolish, feathery, flighty girl who was barely twenty when her father died. Her mother died soon after, possibly from embarrassment, leaving the kingdom, *the Count's kingdom*, in the hands of a girl with no brain at all.

The Queen was admired by all except the Count. The Count knew well that they adored her because she was silly and threw huge and expensive parties where the courtiers were allowed to dance all night. The Count did not dance. Instead, he brooded in a corner of the main ballroom, slumped in his chair, glaring at the rakes and the fops and the low-cut bosoms until his head hurt. He was frequently rude to the Queen, but the Queen was so decidedly silly that she laughed off his uncouth behavior and twirled away for another dance. He had no idea that the Queen was secretly in love with him, and had been since she was fifteen. She was undoubtedly silly, but she loved her Papá, and she loved the Count for loving him too.

For an entire week after he had thought of his mad scheme, the Count spent his days poring over maps and documents and treaties and laws. He counted sums in ledgers of bank accounts that were shrinking in size because of the Queen's wasteful lifestyle. He found one entry extremely galling. The Queen loved to swim, so much so that she had ordered a fountain and a small circular pool installed outside her private chambers, on the second floor of the palace. It was tremendously expensive, and the older members of the court didn't know what to think when the Queen started jumping into the fountain and splashing about like a child. The Count entirely disapproved.

As he stomped around the palace offices, he ignored all queries about his health and his unseemly pallor. When each evening came, and the revels began, he retired to his corner and chewed over the details of his plan. Above all else, the Count was determined that his actions should be patriotic. It was for Queen and Country, after all. Well, not for the Queen, but one shouldn't quibble.

His dear friend Reginald interrupted the Count's gloomy ruminations on a Saturday night around eleven. Reginald was quite drunk, and threw himself down in a chair next to the Count and looked at him with his eyes ever so slightly crossed.

"My dear Count," he asked. "Don't you ever have fun? All you do is sit and stare at the Queen. Are you admiring her bosom?"

"What of it!" the Count rejoined. "Can't a Count stare at a Queen?"

Reginald looked confused. "I don't know. I suppose so," he said. He sat quietly for a few minutes, perhaps because he was trying to think. Reginald was a loyal friend to the Count and of noble birth, but he was remarkably stupid. In fact, he was the Count's only friend, undoubtedly because he wasn't smart enough to know how boring the Count was. That was the whisper murmured when the Count and Reginald were out of earshot. The Count's mother knew better, for she knew that Reginald was a Good Boy. Only a Good Boy would like her son.

Reginald shook his head, unable to think anymore. He looked at the Count and loudly blew his nose.

The Count was too distracted to grind his teeth at Reginald's lack of manners. Instead, he leaned forward and whispered to the younger man.

"Dear boy," he asked. "Are you prepared to die for your country?"

Reginald was drunk but still proud. He saluted automatically and clutched his sword. "You know I am," he replied.

"Dear boy," the Count said again. "Are you prepared to *kill* for your country? To kill an enemy of our fair land? An enemy who is destroying our way of life with pomp and parties and silliness and too much mirth?"

"Yes, sir," Reginald said. He looked sad, especially at the idea of killing mirth, but he was ever loyal to his Count.

The Count smiled, satisfied, and shook Reginald's hand firmly. "Then you are now a member of the Ad Hoc Committee to Kill the Queen. Congratulations! I knew I could count on you."

Reginald's eyes got very wide and, not knowing what else to do, he blew his nose again, for a very long time. The Count restrained himself with an effort. Reginald squirmed in his chair and looked like he wanted to cry. "Not the Queen! I like the Queen!"

The Count shook his head. "Don't worry, Reginald. We will thrust our rapiers into her heart together. She will die quickly. She must die for the Good of the Country. But you cannot back out now. You have already given me your pledge."

Reginald stared at the Count. "I have? I can't back out?"

"No," said the Count. "You cannot. If you do, you will hang as a traitor to the country."

Reginald clutched his neck and loosened his cravat. He had a particular dislike of hanging, coming as he did from a long line of nobles who had been hanged for one reason or another. After gasping for a short while, he looked at the Count and nodded his assent.

The Count slapped him on the back and said, "Buck up, Reg! No one will know. It's not as if this is regicide. She's a Queen, not a King."

"Oh," said Reginald. "Well, I suppose that is all right, then."

❧ ❧ ❧

The next day was Sunday, and the Queen was going to church. She tried to rouse her ladies in waiting, but most of them were suffering from too much drink, and snored through her delicate exclamations of "Wakey, wakey, my little birdies!" Only one girl responded and sleepily followed Her Majesty down the staircase toward the waiting carriage.

The Count watched them from a second-floor window as they walked toward the coach-and-four. He hadn't slept, not even one grim wink of sleep. At 3 a.m., he had escorted Reginald to the Queen's outer chamber and installed him in a closet. Reginald grumbled, for he badly wanted to lie down and sleep, but the Count had insisted. The Count knew how to be strict and had had a great deal of practice beating soldiers over the head with the hilt of his sword. Sometimes he had even used a nearby kettle from a campfire. The Count looked at Reginald sternly and warned him not to kill the Queen before the Count arrived, but to wait for the Count's signal. Reginald had no problem with these instructions and nodded politely. He fell asleep as soon as the Count left the room.

The Count had no thoughts of Reginald now because the Queen was approaching the carriage with her lady-in-waiting. His jaw clenched over and over until he stopped, wincing in pain. Pain, yes. Pain for the Queen. She would go to church and spend exactly one hour. Her return would be swift, and then she would climb the long staircase to her chambers, and then she would die. He would be waiting with Reginald, and the country would be free again. Free from vice and drink and bosoms and fun. Free to have another ruler. One with gravitas. One with sense. Perhaps her uncle. Yes, her uncle would be good. He was immensely fat and smelled and sometimes even broke wind in public. But he was not—definitely not—silly.

A clatter from the drive below brought the Count back to the present. One of the horses from the stables was galloping across the lawn directly toward the carriage. The Count's eyes glinted in expectation. Perhaps a rapier wouldn't be necessary after all. As the horse approached the carriage, a small group of people that had been standing there started to scatter in panic. The Count suddenly clutched the window sill and leaned forward.

"Blast!" he exclaimed. "What are you doing there, Mother?"

It was true. His beloved mother had been waiting for the Queen to emerge from the palace so that she could accompany Her Majesty to church. Now, the elderly woman was just yards away from being struck down and trampled to death. The Count wanted to shout but was too horrified. His mouth opened, but no sound came out. For all of the Count's faults, he loved his mother. She never tired of him, and always embraced him at tea time.

As the Count helplessly watched, he saw the Queen run toward his mother, arms outstretched. With the horse just inches away, rearing up with his hooves ready to strike his mother, the Queen grasped the old woman and ran with her to the other side of the carriage. Seconds later, the horse's hooves pounded into the dirt, and the horse ran again, down the drive toward the gate.

There was quite a lot of noise during the next few moments, with men chasing the horse and men running around the carriage and men cursing and exclaiming and blaming and acting as men often do when a crisis has been averted. Through it all, the Queen was beautiful and calm and not at all silly. She helped the old woman and her trembling lady-in-waiting into the carriage and waved at the courtiers and calmly drove away to church.

The Count was not a religious man, even though he believed in God. It was a requirement for a Count to believe in God, at least if one wanted to be respectable. But on this particular morning, an indefinable unease rumbled through the Count's soul. He stood by the window for the entire time that the Queen was at church, with his hands clenched on the window sill, gazing at the spot where the Queen had saved his mother.

The Count was not a murderer. His determination to kill the Queen had been born from a conviction that the silly girl was ruining his beloved country. As he meditated by the window, he had to admit that she was indeed ruining the country—at least the country's finances. The Count, being a prudent man, hated the idea of anyone ruining their finances. Emptying a country's treasury was tantamount to treason. For this reason, he had justified his plan, believing that history would recognize his patriotism.

Now, after the nobility and self-sacrifice demonstrated by the Queen's rescue of his mother, he found himself helpless in front of his creed. Above all other things, the Count valued heroism. He had seen a quality in the Queen that made him tremble in an agony of self-recrimination. He had been about to kill a rare and noble woman. A silly girl, but a woman of exceptional royalty.

As the coach-and-four swept up the drive, the Count made a decision. He didn't stay to see the Queen descend from the coach and enter the palace. He ran to the hallway outside her chambers and stood there at attention and waited.

The Queen and her lady-in-waiting were laughing merrily as they climbed the staircase to the second floor. As they approached the royal chambers, the Queen saw the Count standing in the middle of the hall, and stopped, puzzled.

"Why, Count! Do you request an audience?"

The Count knelt in front of her and said, "May I speak to you, here, alone?"

The Queen nodded at the lady-in-waiting, who stared curiously at the Count, and then went into the Queen's chambers and closed the door.

"You may speak now, sir," the Queen said.

The Count lowered his forehead until it touched the Queen's shoe. Startled, she stepped back, and exclaimed, "Sir! What is this?"

He straightened but stayed on his knees. As he looked at the Queen, he could barely speak, and much to his surprise, and to the Queen's, he was unable to prevent tears from coming to his eyes.

"Your Majesty, I must beg your forgiveness and ask your mercy."

The Queen's brow was furrowed, and her natural gaiety was gone.

"What do you mean, my dear Count?"

His voice was barely a whisper as he said, "Your Majesty, I love our country. I watched as you saved my mother from death. For that, I owe you my life. I will live for you and die for you, as I did for your father."

Her Majesty had tears in her eyes as she took his hands in hers. "My dear Count! I know how much you loved my father. For that, I love you."

The Count's mad scheme entirely crumbled at her words. His voice was hoarse as he replied, "But you will hate me now, for yesterday I planned to murder you. I thought you would destroy your father's legacy."

The Queen's eyes widened in shock, and she drew her hands back. She stood for a long moment, staring at the Count.

"Lift your head, Count, and look at me, and tell me your intent now."

He lifted his head and gazed at the Queen and said, "You may kill me if you wish. Today I saw that you are your father's daughter. I will serve you with all that I have, and with my life. I only pray for your forgiveness that I misunderstood you."

She looked at him for a very long time, but he didn't move, or squirm, or flinch, or any of the other things a person might do when a Queen is staring at one without blinking. The Count was truly surprised that such a silly girl could stare at him for such a long time. But then he remembered that she wasn't *really* silly—she just acted that way.

After staring at him for such a long time that he was worried that his legs would entirely fall asleep, she sighed, and then sighed again, and then sighed a third time. She stepped closer to him, and took both of his hands in hers, and said, "Dear Count. I have been in love with you since I was fifteen. You have been a grumpy old pinchpenny since my father died, but I am determined to make you laugh. Will you do anything I say, from now on?"

The Count nodded, wondering how the Queen could possibly be in love with him, especially since everyone knew he was bad-tempered and old. Well, not that old. He just felt rather creaky.

The Queen took his chin in her hand and asked, "Will you marry me and be my royal consort?"

His face must have been very comical, for the Queen started laughing. She said again, "Well? Will you?"

All he could say was, "Yes, Your Majesty."

"Good!" she said. She laughed again, one of her most celebrated silly laughs, and pulled him up. His legs were weak, so she put her arm around his waist and guided him to the edge of the fountain that stood outside her door. They sat on the stone ledge for a few minutes, and she just looked at him and smiled. Then, without a bit of warning, she stood up and stepped into the fountain with all of her clothes on, and pulled him in after her, until they were both sitting in the circular pool, with the water up to their chests. Her skirts were billowing around her, and as she squeezed his hand, she laughed and laughed and laughed, until finally, he laughed too.

They made so much noise that the lady-in-waiting opened the door and said, "Your Majesty? Is everything all right?"

The Queen smiled and replied, "Everything is wonderful, my dear. Come, help us out of this pool."

They climbed out of the fountain, and as the Queen walked toward her chambers, the Count darted in front of her and strode into the room, exclaiming, "Your Majesty, we are the Ad Hoc Committee to Save the Queen! We will guard you with our lives!"

The Queen raised a brow and said, "We?"

The Count strode to the door of the closet and said, "Reginald, my friend, was guarding your chambers against any potential assassins." He opened the door and found Reginald sleeping soundly. It took a while to wake him, and when he stirred, he was confused, being Reginald, but there you have it. He finally understood that all was well, and was mightily relieved since he did indeed like the Queen. He bowed and tucked in his shirt and scurried off.

The Count bowed too, and said, "Your Majesty! God bless you."

The Queen smiled and said, "My dear Count! I will see you soon."

❧ ❧ ❧

To say that the kingdom was in an uproar when the news spread that the Queen was to marry the Count, the grim, formal, humorless, boring old Count, was to not understand the levity of the silliest court in all of Europe. Ladies-in-waiting giggled and asked all types of questions. Courtiers drank themselves into mournful stupors because they had wanted to marry the Queen.

It wasn't until the Queen and the Count had been married for a number of months that everyone settled down. A curious change had swept over the court. It had become just a little bit more sensible. There were still parties and dancing and bosoms and fun. The Queen insisted that fun would never be outlawed. Much to his surprise, the Count thoroughly agreed with his newfound love. The silliest, but also the noblest Queen in the world, had taught the Count how to laugh. Her spirit and beauty and love had melted him. She even appealed to his sense of truth by saying, "Darling, don't you know that God is the one who invented laughter? Why else would He have created monkeys and giraffes?"

The Count could say nothing to refute her most impeccable logic. So he lent her his wisdom and prudence and loyalty and bravery, and discovered that the silliest girl in the land was his heroine and his partner, and very good for the kingdom after all.

The courtiers and ladies-in-waiting never knew that the Ad Hoc Committee to Save the Queen saved a Count and a Kingdom and a Queen, all because of a runaway horse.

The Count and the Queen grew very fond of that horse and named it Reginald.

The Day I Said No
to Kim Jong Un

"*Y*ou. Attend to me."

Kim Jong Un had almost brushed past me as he walked through the conference room, surrounded by his security men. I'm not sure why, but he stopped and stared at me for a moment before he spoke.

His security men didn't give me a chance to reply, as one of them took my arm and led me out of the room behind the Supreme Leader. I glanced back at the people in the hall, wondering if I would see them again.

I had been in South Korea many times, but this was my first time in North Korea. I had come as part of a delegation of three men from the United States to an international conference that was classified and unreported. All I can say about it is that the majority of attendees didn't like Kim and he didn't like us. Privately, we exchanged barbs about him, calling him "His Chubbiness" and "Cannon Meister." When we met him, of course, we were all smiles. I spoke Korean, which put me at some advantage since I didn't have to rely on translators who often lied. My team's mission was simple, but not something one wanted to attempt unless one was certifiable. We needed to convince the Fat One that we hated the United States and wanted to help him in his megalomaniacal schemes. After that, we would be a fount of false information. Utterly deniable by anyone in the State Department. Of course. We believed in our mission—at least I know that I did. I didn't like the idea of Little Boots II bringing down our electric grid with EMP nukes.

Our primary tactic was to schmooze him and get him to believe that we were totally committed to support him and adore him and help him in every way. We doubted that he would trust our overtures, but we had to try. So, we clapped at his rancid jokes and praised his collection of fast cars and told him as many nice things as we could invent at short notice. I might have overdone it, for here I was, taken in tow behind him as the conference room door closed with a thud.

To my relief, I wasn't ushered to the fourth subbasement of the Pyongyang palace to be slowly tortured. Instead, as we walked to his private quarters, he took my hand in his overly soft paw and whispered, "You must teach me all about the vices of America. I adore videos of women. Many women. All at once."

My Adam's apple moved quite substantially as I swallowed, and said, "Of course, Dear Leader."

The next few days were difficult for me. I didn't like videos like that at all. Not even a little bit. They made me feel greasy, and my pores felt clogged with cement. Fortunately, I was able to avert my eyes most of the time, with the excuse that I had to explore other vices for him to enjoy.

I had learned in my time in Korea that some Korean men think that the universe started its revolution of stars and planets when they were born and that the sun would never go to bed unless they graciously gave it leave to depart. Not all Korean men, mind you. Some were fabulous and warm and humorous and would drop everything and walk you to your destination if you asked them for directions.

No, I'm talking about Men of Hubris, who, of course, can be found all over the world. These men take inordinate satisfaction in watching people bow and scrape and proffer their souls and fortunes for the pleasures of the leader.

His Squirminess was such a man, a man whom Lord Acton could point to and thunder, "Harumph! I told you that power corrupts! Now, do you believe me?"

I believed him. Yes, I did. Kim Jong Un was just about the most corrupted man of absolute power that I had ever met. When I managed to slip away one afternoon and catch up with my two companions, they told me that the conference attendees had started a wager to see who could figure out how many communicable diseases Kim had picked up in his bed-hopping adventures. The odds were on "more than twenty."

The conference was one of those hunkered-down, month-long affairs that managed to keep its participants because of all the after-hours thrills. In North Korea, good-times were limited to a microscopic area of Pyongyang, serviced by a population handpicked to make Westerners think that everyone in North Korea was as fat as His Plumpness and happier than anyone could possibly be. No one believed that, but the more scurrilous conference members didn't care anyway. They just wanted to have fun.

My two partners were delighted that I had made a breakthrough with Kim and encouraged me to keep at it and "attend" him. So I did.

KJU was fascinated with his own brilliance, and to help him think that I was too, I shadowed him continuously. As he weaved his way through the conference, graciously smiling at leaders from around the world, I walked one step behind him, with my notebook and pen ready to take down his instructions. I made sure to bend over slightly so that my six-foot-two frame was less conspicuous next to His Shrimpiness.

Following him around was a hard task, and left me no freedom to talk with other conference-goers. I felt especially chagrined as a friend— a tall and lanky Anglican vicar—bustled up to me as I was following Kim through a revolving door into a fake French restaurant. I waved my hand at him and shook my head, and plunged on through, barely hearing the vicar's words, "I just have one question!"

Leaving Kim's side was simply not an option if my mission was to succeed.

By the fifth day of my devotion to the Great Leader, things were going well. Kim seemed to be interested in me as a person. He told me that I wouldn't be required at the next morning's 5 a.m. staff meeting because I looked tired. I thanked him and said that, yes, I was plagued with headaches every day, and, in fact, had one at that very moment.

He looked at me curiously and said, "Oh, you too? What do you do about them? I have headaches sometimes, and my physician says it's too much stress. So I usually just find a relative or friend and shoot them with my cannon. It's amazing! The headaches just go away. Maybe they're afraid of me."

His method was a high bar to surmount, so I simply said, "Well, I usually breathe hard, and lean against a wall. Hopefully, not in front of a cannon."

His face got red for a moment, and I thought I wasn't going to have to worry about headaches any longer, but then he burst out laughing and slapped his knee. He looked around at his security men and the gaggle of half-dressed women who were all nervously staring at their feet and bellowed, "In front of a cannon! Did you hear that! This American is really stupid, but I like him anyway."

He kept going back to it over the next few days, muttering "in front of a cannon!" and then giggling to himself.

I was gaining his trust, it seemed to me, with every apple that I polished. At one point, he brought out a boxed set of DVDs to show to some of the European conference members and said, "These are great videos of women divers. You should all watch them."

The Germans and French seemed mildly interested, but the folks from the Vatican had to act respectable, so they shook their heads and went back to their discussion about why North Korean noodles were inferior. His Sweetness puffed out his chest, which was farther back than his stomach, and was about to order his cannon, so I thought I'd better step in and save the Vatican.

"You know, Dear Leader, that we should show these videos of women divers to all of the participants at today's plenary session. And then, we can do a Q&A with you leading the program. I think that would be very grand. Don't waste them on this small group of ignoramuses. I think your idea to do this for the whole group is brilliant."

Since I said all of this in Korean, the Europeans just smiled, and the Vatican men shrugged and lit their cigars. But Kim: oh my, he was so pleased with himself that he waved away the cannon man and ordered extra lunch for everyone.

The next day—a Friday—Kim came and roused me out of bed and said that I had to drive with him to the airport. He was on his way to his private island, where he went whenever he felt the need for *really* secret vices. He went there about once a week.

Before we left, I told my two teammates to meet me at the Pyongyang Supreme Leader's Number One Bulgogi Restaurant, where we could catch up and have some lunch. I was feeling draggy around the edges with all of the scurrying and scraping.

I sat in the front of the Chinese-made limousine, and Kim and two of his mistresses sat in the back. It didn't take long to get to the airport across the empty roads, since nobody could afford cars except members of the government and the military.

At the airport, I helped him out of the limo, giving him my arm to get out. His legs were hurting, probably because of gout and his evil ways. After he straightened up, I glanced back in the car and saw that he had dropped his wallet and sunglasses, so I leaned in and got them. He seemed grateful.

He was turning away, with a woman on each arm, but then he stopped and looked at me.

"You have to do something for me."

I bowed, and said, "Of course, Great Leader."

He put on his sunglasses and said, "You have to kill someone. At least one person. I don't care who it is. But you have to kill one person before I come back on Monday. Or even two or three. But not too many. You have to leave some for me. I need to know that you're with me."

Not knowing how to work this new turn of events, I simply said, "Yes, Dear Leader. Of course. Have a lovely time."

He snorted and turned away, with his babes on his arms, who both looked back at me as if to say, "You stupid American. You should have stayed at home."

I stubbed my toe, getting back into the limo, and asked the driver to drop me at the restaurant, which he did. He looked at me like I was a moron. Maybe I was. For a few minutes, I couldn't even remember how to say moron in Korean.

My buddies jumped up when I approached their corner table. They must have noticed my white face, or perhaps it was my trembling lips or my deep sighs of Get Me Outa Here angst. Whatever it was, they plied me with bulgogi and kimchee and sparkling cider and then even more kimchee. The kimchee helped a lot. When a person feels weak in the pit of his stomach, kimchee will fix him right up. I've always felt that Koreans personify bulgogi and kimchee in their spirit and character and personality. Not wimpy at all.

But every time I thought about the Royal Command that His Putrescence had given me, I felt sick. My companions wisely took me out to the empty streets of Pyongyang, where we could commiserate and curse the Cannon Meister without anyone hearing us.

They wanted me to go through with it. "Think of the mission," they said. "Think of the millions of lives saved from EMP attacks."

I couldn't argue with anything they said, but I told them that I needed to be alone. So they obligingly left me to my own devices. I wandered the streets of Pyongyang for several enervating hours until soldiers stopped me from going out of the "posh" areas. Eventually, I found a taxi and went back to the hotel.

Saturday and Sunday were hard days. I won't tell you what I did, but you know, a man's gotta do what a man's gotta do. Like they say in Texas. Or is it Connecticut? I'm not sure. I felt cornered and mumbled over and over, "Whaddya gonna do?" *That's* from New Jersey. I know that for a fact.

On Monday, around 9 a.m., the Roly-Poly Tyrant called me into his penthouse office that looked out over the hollow grandeur of a miserable city. His office had sliding windows that opened onto a massive, terraced balcony upon which he hosted mandatory dance parties, set to the music of the Beach Boys.

He stood up when I came in and motioned for me to follow him onto the terrace. I did, trying to figure out his mood.

He led me to a corner of the terrace and looked me up and down.

"Well?" he asked.

I bowed carefully. "Dear Leader, I believe that you need men whom you can trust because they never lie to you."

He nodded and murmured something.

"Well, I am that kind of valuable man. I'm happy to report that I'm a man of principle that you can count on."

"How many?" he asked.

I stood a little straighter and replied, "I cannot kill anyone, Dear Leader, because that would go against my principles. And you wouldn't want that, would you?"

He glared at me and then punched me in the chest and ranted and shrieked and cursed and spat. It was both amazing to behold and boring since I had seen so many Korean men do the same, although not with the panache of the Bilious Brat.

"You really are a stupid American! I didn't want to have to use my cannon, because you helped me learn all about the naked women of America even more than I knew already." He leered and then preened. "And, of course, I know everything."

He pointed behind me. "Make a choice. Kill someone like I said, or . . ."

He stopped and looked at a piece of paper in his hand. "Oh yes, that's it . . . say hello to my little friend!"

I turned around and, yes, indeed, his little friend was there, but it wasn't little at all. In the opposite corner of the terrace sat a gold-plated cannon, with a swimsuit-clad girl standing next to it with a long-handled lighter.

The Supreme Leader of the Democratic People's Republic of Korea walked with dignified and unhurried steps and put his arm around the cannon girl, who smiled at him, probably hoping that she would not be next.

The Big Boss looked at me and said, "Here's a bit more incentive. We have agents in your capitalist pig of a country, and if you don't kill someone, our agents will kill your entire family, including your wife, your children, your three sisters, and your aged grandmother. It's up to you."

I looked at the Horrid Leader, and then gazed at the overcast pallor of the North Korean sky, and then at the reluctant slip of a cannon girl, and thought for a long moment. I had always felt critical when I saw the tired old movie plot where you have the bomber moan to the FBI that he *had* to blow up the office building and kill all of the people inside because the terrorists had kidnapped his family and if he didn't do it, the terrorists were going to kill his family. So he had no choice.

I always thought, well, of course he had a choice. Better to die and have his family die, proud of him to the last because he had not murdered other innocent people on their account.

And here I was, on the horns of the same dilemma.

I looked at Kim—the mean-as-a-snake, doomed Kim Jong Un—and said, "No."

The Cannon Meister scowled. He hated it when people said no. Then he smiled, quite happily it seemed, and motioned to the cannon girl.

I don't remember what happened after that.

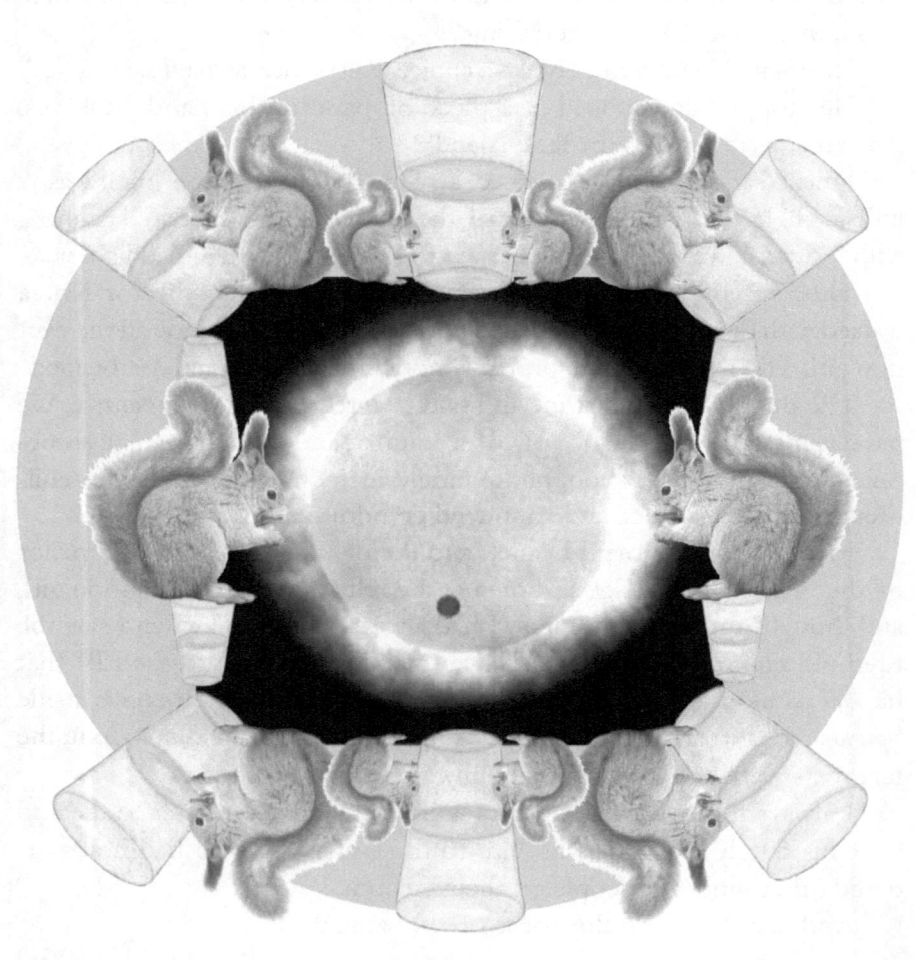

The Epiphany of
Zebediah Clump

Zebediah Clump was doomed. Knowing this, his interest in life had taken a sharp left turn into the toilet of resentful destiny. All that was good was flushed away.

He had never been a happy man. Aging, overweight, and bald, Zebediah had spent decades drinking from a glass that was half empty. Every bird dropping that fell on his fine new automobile convinced him that Chicken Little was a depressingly prescient bird of death.

Reading the newspaper was an agonizing experience for Zebediah— a flagellation of drooling and wild-eyed anxiety about events beyond his control. The world was collapsing, and Zebediah was sinking with it.

His spiral into gloom accelerated in the year 2012. Watching doomsday films cemented his opinion of the future into a certainty of bitter resignation that life would end within the year. He pored through scientific tomes that were priced by the pound but found nothing to alleviate his grim despair. He cursed in

an unfamiliar tongue when he found that he wouldn't even live until December 21, the Mayan date of the end of the world.

As was his habit, he had expertly discovered information that was worse than he had expected. He had thought that the winter solstice might be a relatively cool way to die, bundled up in a blanket, waiting for his blood to slowly freeze as he fell asleep. But no, life was cruel—cruel and mean and dastardly. He, with all of the souls lost in the tracks of the mortal coil, would not even last until the summer solstice. Death would arrive early, on June 5, 2012, as the planet Venus meandered its way across the face of the sun.

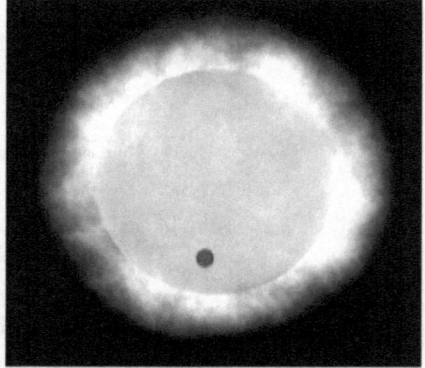

His spiritualist sister attempted to convince him that he was wrong—that the Venus Transit was a time of expanded communication—a time of awakened consciousness. He argued and shouted and banged the phone on the tabletop, ignoring her ministrations. He felt sorry for his sister, and her pathetic attempt to feel hopeful. He knew better because he knew that a planetary alignment of such magnitude was Very Bad News. He didn't know why he knew, but knowing why was unimportant for a man whose glass was half empty.

With the confirmation of his fate, Zebediah descended into a fog of resigned ennui. Each moment of every day resembled the last and the next—puddles of gray befuddlement that splashed across his unwashed clothes, leaving an aroma of disgust trailing behind him as he stumbled from room to room. Zebediah had become blind to the beauty of a day.

Flowers meant nothing to him. Admiring his favorite tree was something he might have done before; now, he kicked it and muttered imprecations. Standing by the kitchen windows, he spied a bird happily pecking for seeds on the railing of his porch. He scowled at the bird, peeved that his sister had put out more seeds when global destruction would soon obliterate the planet.

Squirrels came and went, and flicked their fluffy tails, but were regarded without a single smile.

In Zebediah's world, cuteness was thoroughly dead.

In the darkened mind of Z. Clump, the tiny and seemingly insignificant movement of the planet Venus across the face of the sun was an event that reduced his body to a quivering jelly of unkempt terror. He spent the day of June 5 curled on his bed in the fetal position, whimpering.

He didn't see the planet Venus that evening. He didn't sense the ripples of its transit curling across his body, loosening the grout lodged in the fluting of his heart.

Instead, he waited for the morning, and death, and the final depletion of his half-empty glass. As he waited, he growled. And wept. But nothing happened at all. Death failed to arrive.

After waiting for quite a considerable time, the fetal position became very uncomfortable, even for a man who was determined to be depressed. Uncurling his stiffened limbs with a groan, Zebediah stood up and limped downstairs to the kitchen.

He felt dazed to see the morning light and didn't know what to make of the fact that he wasn't dead. He stood at the kitchen window, wondering what had happened to the planet Venus, and the sun, and the earth, for that matter.

Sipping a glass of water, he stared at a squirrel nibbling seeds on the railing. It was a lovely squirrel with an exceptionally bold tail. The squirrel looked at Zebediah, and he looked at it.

They exchanged glance after glance, back and forth, and back again, until Zebediah suddenly realized that he was having give and take with a squirrel—something that depressed individuals rarely found worthwhile.

He wasn't sure how the chuckle started, but, quite suddenly, a short little chortle slipped out of his mouth, rather like an embarrassing burp. It surprised him so much that he opened his mouth and started to laugh. He found his laugh so amusing that he decided that he would continue with the strange phenomenon, and laughed again, and then again.

Soon the kitchen was filled with the sound of Zebediah Clump laughing. He had to lean against the counter to stop himself from spilling his water glass. It was the strangest thing. He scratched his head in confusion, not knowing why he laughed. It might have been relief that he hadn't died as Venus traveled in its orbit across the sun. But then . . . perhaps doomsday was still on course, honing in on his tremulous existence as he sipped his water and looked at a squirrel.

As he rubbed his temple, he realized that it didn't matter anymore. Doomsday, shoomsday. What could anyone do about it?

Taking his water glass with him, he decided on a whim to check his mailbox. Was it the influence of the Venus Transit that inspired him to go outside? He didn't know, but as he stood on his porch, he noticed that he was breathing. Breathing was good.

Breathing was good even when a bird once again christened his lovely new van with a loud plop. Zebediah Clump stared at the offending spot of white on the windshield and just breathed.

Breathing was indeed a gratifying activity. He was turning to enter his home when he paused and noticed the tree—the lonely tree—the tree that might have been sad when he kicked it.

He was quite surprised that he felt sympathetic toward the tree and almost ignored his feelings. Instead, he walked to the tree and kissed it. Yes, indeed, Z. Clump kissed a tree, right on its gnarly bark, in plain view of the neighbors, under a sky filled with birds that loved his automobile far more than was good for it.

As he raised his water glass to salute the tree, Zebediah noticed a very curious thing. Even though he had taken many a sip of water on that fine summer morning, his glass was still half full.

In 2011, *The Epiphany of Zebediah Clump*
was made into an 8½-minute film.

It went on to win the Best "Short Narrative" Film Award
at the Portland Maine Film Festival in 2012.

It was also nominated for "Best Maine Film"
at the Sanford International Film Festival in 2015.

You can view the film at
worldcommunitypress.com/clump

The Day the Moon Smiled

The Master of the Moon was just finishing a detailed sketch of a dimple when the light over the message tube flashed red. He paused and thoughtfully erased a smudge on the paper, trying to ignore the insistent flashing. He had been expecting it for days.

He had posed a query to his helpers, all of whom were geniuses in the mathematics of probability and behavior. His question was direct and simple but had caused a tremendous commotion within his staff. There was a great scurrying back and forth between calculators and printouts, with thousands of pages covering desks and floors. Discussions commenced, fingers were counted, and even crystal balls were consulted.

He understood their angst because he already knew the answer. In spite of that, he wanted them to participate in the decision, and thus, the question had to be asked. He had written it down and had directed that it be distributed to everyone, even to the most junior members. Most of them had to read it several times:

"Should I make the face happy or sad?"

His helpers were beings of exceptional sympathy, and the thought of a sad face peering down from the moon seemed so final and so tragic that some of them hid in closets or went promptly to bed and cried without a single thought of sleep. They had worked with the Master for such a very long time, creating atoms and molecules and planets and solar systems, all as preparation to build a home on the earth for the Master's lovely children. So much still had to be done: dinosaurs and mountain lions; tulips and tree frogs; raccoons and hummingbirds; puppies and kittens; and, of course, after all of that, the very first human beings.

The older staff members had to help their younger partners face the disheartening but unavoidable truth that giving humans free will would immediately stack the odds against them. It was a wonderful gift that would allow them to eventually grow and mature into glorious beings of love. But the cost would be bitter, for a person who is free to love is also free to descend into savagery and bloodshed. The human journey would be long and painful.

As the Master smoothed out the message on the worktable, his hand trembled, knocking over a jar of ink, blotting out the drawing on the table. The note was terse. "We're so very sorry. We think it must be sad."

❧ ❧ ❧

During the next few years, the studio floating high above the earth lay abandoned. A deathlike atmosphere of gloom crawled along the floor, swirling around the vacant chairs and easels. The drawing of the dimpled face lay discarded on the table, its smile hidden by the caked India ink. Dust lay everywhere.

When the door finally creaked open, the drawing had yellowed, and the paper had become brittle. The Master of the Moon hardly glanced at it, brushing it aside in a puff of dust. His assistant, a tall and quiet-faced person, watched sadly as the drawing fluttered to the floor, lodging behind a high-backed chair.

The Master glanced at the assistant. "Come now. Leave it there. The moon will have a face very soon."

With a sigh, the assistant nodded and placed a new sheet of clean paper on the table. He bit his lip slightly as he laid out a set of quill pens and opened a jar of ink. Striding to the windows, he threw open the shutters, allowing the light of the moon to come streaming through the studio. He gazed at the surface of the moon. Except for a variety of small craters from colliding meteors, it was a shiny white stone, waiting for a personality.

The assistant spoke diffidently. "You will not use the other sketch, Master? It was such a delightful, happy face. Would your children on the earth not be inspired by it, as they struggle in their pain?"

The Master nodded. "Yes, of course they would." His pen was busy, making clean, broad strokes on the paper. He looked at his assistant, calmly. "You are forgetting, my friend, how far away they will become."

The Master carefully added a bit of shading around the mouth. "The violence of their passions will drive many of them into a darkness that will block all knowledge of us from their hearts and minds. The spark of love will eventually guide them, but it will take millennia for that to happen."

The assistant shuddered. He didn't want to contemplate the reality of the Master's words and was astonished at the tranquility in his voice.

He moved closer to the table and stared down at the face that had taken shape under the Master's hand.

"It is such a sad face."

The Master didn't answer as he looked at the sketch. Satisfied, he blew on the paper to dry the ink and then briskly rolled up the drawing. He handed it to the assistant, with a nod toward the message tube on the wall. The assistant inserted it into the tube and pressed a button. With a whoosh, the drawing was gone.

The Master motioned the assistant to the window, where they both leaned against the windowsill and gazed at the surface of the moon. As they watched, a stream of asteroids came into view, moving at great speed toward the moon. First one, then a dozen, and finally hundreds crashed into its untouched skin, flinging gigantic clouds of powder and debris across its surface.

As the last asteroid hit the surface, flashes of red light spread across the impact craters, cracking open the stony surface. Lava welled up from the fissures, filling in the craters and spreading across the moon's expanse.

The assistant gazed in awe as the face that the Master had drawn on paper slowly appeared on the surface of the moon. Finally, the massive flow of lava stopped, and the moon was once again silent and shining.

The Master pointed to the earth, floating serenely below the moon. "Someday, some of my children will stare up at the surface of the moon, and see that sad face, and ask why it is so mournful. They'll ask themselves how it came to be, and they'll argue about craters and asteroids and random mathematics. Eventually, they'll realize that chance had nothing to do with it, for what are the chances that unthinking rocks could carve a face like their own?"

The assistant nodded. "Then they'll remember you. I see."

The Master placed his hand on the assistant's shoulder. "Yes. And perhaps they'll wonder how I feel."

"Master?" the assistant asked.

"Yes?"

"Why do you not draw a face upon the other side? It is rather drab, is it not?"

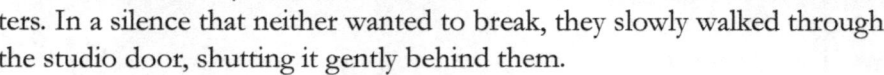

"Yes, it is. But they will not be able to see the other side from where they stand."

They stood for a while, gazing at the sad face of the moon. Finally, the assistant closed the shutters. In a silence that neither wanted to break, they slowly walked through the studio door, shutting it gently behind them.

The face on the moon kept watch as the Master and his helpers prepared the earth for humans. Three and a half billion years passed as they designed and developed a vast array of species of life. Despite the moon's silent reminder of the future of his children, the Master encouraged his charges to enjoy their work, for was it not endlessly fascinating to create living organisms like moss piglets and proboscis monkeys? His helpers could not but agree, and continued their work.

They were thrilled and then dismayed as they watched the first humans multiply in number. The Master's prophecy proved correct. Once enlightened children slid down into a brutish existence, punctuated by the gnawing of bones and howling in the dark. Many things escaped their notice, such as the niceties of bathing and the brushing of one's teeth. They had no knowledge of tools and fire-building. The concepts of science and the realms of higher thought were absent for a very long time. When they met each other, they were only dimly aware that they were different from the animals that they eagerly hunted for their next meal. Huddled together for warmth on cold nights, they stared up at the moon and thought that it was a god. They scrabbled at the bottom of human existence.

In those days, the Master of the Moon never visited the studio. He and his assistants spent most of their time monitoring his children on the planet. His assistants were awed by his patience, and privately wondered how many millennia it would take to bring knowledge to the earth. When they became impatient with the dullness of their human charges, they gazed upward at the sad face of the moon and silently continued their work. Yet, more than once, they grew discouraged because of the darkness of that time. Goodness seemed entirely extinct.

The Master of the Moon shared many of their feelings. As his assistants brought him the recorded volumes of each year, he would often leave them unopened on their shelves. He knew their contents, and reviewing them again was too painful, for every page was drenched with the blood of his children. Instead, he reminded his assistants that no deed or thought, no matter how dreadful, could destroy the beautiful core of heart inside each of his children. It was that core that they labored to find in their travels upon the earth.

As time passed, bright spots gradually appeared among the masses of his troubled children. His assistants eagerly told him about each new man or woman or child they found who thought and felt in a new way, a kind and more loving way, leaving behind the callousness of their neighbors. A team of helpers was immediately dispatched to guide and protect each of those illuminated individuals. Protecting them was difficult, for their neighbors had the unfortunate habit of murdering them as quickly as they could, for illumination was not popular.

The Master and his helpers grieved when a person's beautiful light on the earth was snuffed out in a barbarous attack. They welcomed each individual to their final home with the comforting assurance that with martyrdom, all was not lost.

An ever-expanding atmosphere of goodness was being created by thousands of acts of kindness, love, and sacrifice on the part of his children. Knowledge was enveloping the earth. The Master and his assistants gave special attention to the few, great individuals who, by their extraordinary examples, were helping to wrestle humanity from the primeval mud.

The assistants reported with amusement that the moon had become a prominent figure in popular culture. They related with some glee that "the Man in the Moon" had entered the public lexicon, and had appeared in many children's stories. The Master of the Moon gently reminded them that such things were all well and good, but had anyone yet wondered why the Man in the Moon wasn't smiling? They bowed their heads and could not answer. He reassured them and told them to wait and be patient. The sphere of love growing in the world had already achieved an unstoppable momentum.

The Master of the Moon had, at long last, achieved remarkable success. Civilization had arrived in most corners of the world. Having guided many of his children to become teachers and prophets and saints, he was overjoyed by reports that violence and hatred were on the decline. There were still outbreaks of strife, and many of them were dreadful in the extreme. His assistants frequently marveled at his endurance and vitality. It was merely that, compared to the dark brutality of the past, the Master knew that an irreversible illumination of the human soul had begun.

The methods that he used to reclaim the human heart were frequently obscure. Untangling the pain and resentment and evil actions of history were jobs that his assistants had obediently left to him. In return, he insisted that he had always been powerless without the response of all those whose hearts had been touched. Compelling humans to love would have removed their free will, and with that, their destiny as beings who would one day resonate and commune with the source of love.

Thus, he had forced himself to wait. Even now, at the final hour, he waited. He was not idle, for there were many things that he could do, many ways that he and his helpers could assist in the process of reclamation. He felt as if he were running a graduate school, desperately anxious for his best students to win their doctorates. He had taught his children about love according to their cultures and had managed to inspire millions upon millions of students, all specializing in their particular branches of knowledge. His children were doing well and some had made tremendous progress. The Master was proud of them, but knowing that a race was not won until the end, he refused to rest. His assistants were particularly solicitous in those final days, taking great care to report every instance of victory on the earth.

Later, his assistants would remark among themselves that the final steps of their labors had seemed the longest, probably because they were all at their most anxious. A great transformation had swept across the earth after the most prominent thinkers of the age had finally cast aside their conflicting viewpoints and had agreed to adopt a commonsense view of human affairs. Peace began slowly at first and then gathered so much momentum that the twenty-four-hour news channels had to add staff to keep up with the stories of inspiration. So much reasonableness overwhelmed some media pundits, who had been prone to report the darker side of life in order to gain viewers and increase their ratings.

Children were the ultimate beneficiaries, for the grownups finally realized that they had to teach children everywhere that they were all connected to a gigantic powerhouse of love that had unfortunately been ignored for far too long. The children didn't mind hearing such things, and great masses of children managed to remember who they really were, even as they traversed the rocky slopes of adolescence. A tidal wave of change had finally swept across the world.

The Master was particularly pleased when his tall and quiet assistant carefully placed in front of him the front pages of newspapers from around the globe. At the top of each, with a banner headline, was a story about the sad face of the moon. A distinguished panel of scholars had met and had concluded that asteroids and volcanoes needed more than random mathematics to carve out faces in planetary objects. Someone rather erudite had mentioned that they had never been able to get a monkey to randomly type out *Romeo and Juliet*. The group had thus reached the inevitable determination that a Great Consciousness must have deliberately carved the face in the moon. They had added an addendum, in bold letters, at the end of the last paragraph of their wordy and sophisticated analysis. It stated, quite simply: "We got the message. We know why it's sad. Can you fix it?"

The next day, the assistant had to call three of his strongest aides to help him push the door of the studio open. The studio hadn't been used for such a long time that it took them half an hour of earth time to fully open the door. The assistant immediately rushed to the windows and opened the shutters, letting in the cool night air. He watched approvingly as a junior aide brought in a cart filled with flowers. After a few moments, the studio had taken on a fresh, new atmosphere. Pressing the button of an intercom, the assistant spoke quickly, unable to contain his excitement. "We're ready."

A moment later, the Master of the Moon entered, smiling broadly. He looked at his assistant. "Did you find it?"

The assistant pointed to the table. "Yes, sir. I've cleaned it up. It's ready to go."

The Master strode to the table and looked down at the drawing of the smiling face that had lain hidden for so long, half-forgotten under a chair. His assistant had worked wonders, removing, through a complicated process, all traces of spilled ink and yellowing from age. It looked as though it had been drawn that very day.

The Master looked around at the group of waiting assistants. He smiled again, and they all smiled back. He took a long, feathery quill pen and gently dipped it into a bottle of India ink. With the utmost care, slowly, hiding the trembling of his hand, he wrote the word "Approved" at the bottom of the drawing.

He placed the pen on the table and rolled up the drawing. Handing it to the assistant, he smiled once more. The room broke into a tumult of cheers. The assistant couldn't speak, for tears were streaming down his face as he gently inserted the rolled drawing into the message tube and pushed the button.

The Master of the Moon, who understood such feelings, put his arm around the assistant and motioned everyone to the windows, where they stood transfixed as a stream of white and gray asteroids descended upon the moon. The assistant watched in fascination as the asteroids hit just the right spots in the dark lava fields, creating a thick, sticky powder as they exploded, hiding long sections of the mournful image.

It was over in a few minutes. Squinting his eyes in order to see the face at a distance, the Master turned to the group of assistants. The tall assistant swore later that he saw a grin ripple across his face, as the Master of the Moon asked the room at large, "Is it okay?"

His children on the earth spent many years after that, talking about the day the moon smiled. It was universally acknowledged that although the Mona Lisa was indeed a great work of art, it lacked the grandeur and the subtlety of the smile on their very own three-dimensional postcard from the Master of the Moon.

Photo of far side of the moon by NASA

"The lunar far side lacks the large, dark, basaltic plains, or maria, that are so prominent on the Earth-facing side."

"This image shows the far side of the moon, illuminated by the sun, as it crosses between the DSCOVR spacecraft's Earth Polychromatic Imaging Camera (EPIC) camera and telescope, and the Earth—one million miles away."

NASA's Goddard Space Flight Center
Greenbelt, MD, USA, August 5, 2015

The Captive

orty-thousand years ago, surrounded by outcroppings of rock, there lived a small tribe of thoroughly unkempt individuals who spent their time hunting for birds and gambling for slaves. One of those slaves, known only as Limp, was breathing heavily as he pressed himself against the cliff under their encampment and peered at the jagged rocks below.

He tried to ignore the death that awaited him and instead took solace in the thought that his recent capture had given him the chance to prevent his friend from being ordered over the cliff. She was too small and weak to have survived.

His captors didn't mind forcing Limp over the cliff's edge instead of the girl. Slaves were easy to obtain. When two or three of the men of the group felt bored, they would hoist themselves erect and announce to their fellows that they would soon return with a new prize whom they could all kick and slap and even, if they were lucky, induce to work.

There were always tasks to be done in their settlement. Their dwellings were shallow caves in the side of a mountain, recessed behind a platform of granite upon which they gathered to argue and curse and chew on birds that their slaves or women cooked on the common fire.

The slaves did most of the labor, giving the women time to hang on the necks of the men and hiss complaints about their slaves and demand better ones. The slaves were always busy with the preparation of roasted birds or the endless task of throwing distasteful items from the cliff's edge to the rocks below. There simply wasn't room on their little plateau for anything unnecessary, which included slaves who didn't work and other types of waste.

The leader of the band was a corpulent collection of vanity and scars—tattoos of conquests and sketches scraped off that were best forgotten. When he stood one day and spat in the direction of his favorite hangers-on, he almost tripped over a slave girl.

He growled and kicked her and then promptly forgot all about her. It was time to venture out once more, up the mountain along secret pathways and tunnels and then over the top to a land beyond in which slaves could be won, if the gambling bones were thrown just right.

He left with his men, sent off with malodorous kisses from the women and the banging of sticks and howls from their children. The slaves looked at each other and sadly whispered the hope that the men would have no luck at all on their journey.

The slave girl whom the leader had kicked was still young enough to have a flash of brightness in her eyes. If the layers of dirt had been washed off, she would have been jealously described by the women as "not as ugly as some." But she did indeed have an excessively dirty face, so much so that she had earned the name "Dirty Nose."

She had been brought to the camp when she was a child and had spent many nights crying for her mother. Over the years, she had demonstrated unusual traits. Many of the slaves, beset as they were by the pressure to survive at any cost, gave little thought to the trials of their companions. They were invariably surprised when she tended to the slaves who were beaten or molested by the members of the tribe.

She had learned to avoid the caves after her body matured. The greasiest of the men vied for her and demanded that the leader give her to them. The leader would cuff them and shout that he was saving her. Thus, she had avoided being taken by any of them, unlike the other, more unfortunate slave girls.

Still, she would retreat to the cliff's edge to avoid the men, for she had discovered that the members of the tribe were afraid of the land below. When they threw bones and refuse over the cliff, they did so from many feet back, and when they saw her sitting on the edge, swinging her legs back and forth without a care, they growled and screamed in anger and terror.

Something dreadful had happened; that she knew. One night, after the men had feasted and drunk until they were almost unconscious, one of the men had started shouting about the monsters in the water— dreadful, dark beasts that had eaten the women of their tribe. The other men joined in and told tales of how young girls would climb down the cliff and disappear forever. None of the tribe knew when the events had occurred, but it was long ago, before the births of their grandfathers.

Dirty Nose listened and marveled, and would often sit at the cliff's edge, searching for monsters. She could see that the land below was not that far away, perhaps about the same distance as the world above where she had come from, carried through pathways and tunnels when she was a small girl.

At the bottom of the cliff, there was a long strip of what looked to her like sand, next to a vast expanse of ocean that stretched to the edge of the world. She had never seen water like that and didn't know what to make of it. For all her watching, though, she never saw any dark shapes moving across the surface.

When she asked one of the slaves about the monsters, the old woman looked at her piteously and sucked on her teeth.

"Dirty Nose, you will meet them soon enough."

The girl looked confused. "What do you mean, grandmother?"

The woman pointed at the rocks above their camp. "The leader always looks to the water when he returns from the land above, and if he sees the monsters, he does what has always been done."

"What is that?"

The slave woman sighed. "I have never seen it, and I have been here for a long time. But I was told by an old woman, when I was a child, that the only way to stop the monsters from climbing up our cliff and devouring us all is to give them what they come for."

Dirty Nose looked at the woman, who was staring at the ground, and began to feel afraid. "What do the monsters come for, grandmother?"

The woman looked up and stared sadly at Dirty Nose. "For a young girl like you, my child. For you. That is why the leader is saving you. For when the monsters return. You will climb down the cliff and give yourself to them, to devour you."

Dirty Nose started to tremble and cry as the old woman took her in her arms and stroked her hair.

"There, there, my girl. I am sorry."

She rested in the old woman's embrace as she cried. Even though death was unremarkable—even ordinary—for slaves, Dirty Nose felt a sense of overwhelming panic as she imagined the monsters' teeth ripping into her flesh. Underneath her panic, she felt something else stir, an angry, resolute glimmer of a thought that she would not let it happen.

After a long while, she stood up and kissed the woman's cheek and thanked her. The old woman tried to smile but could not.

Dirty Nose went about her duties over the next few months, wondering when she would have to climb down the cliff to a gruesome end. She had seen death more than once on the plateau. Two slaves had tried to escape one night and were caught in the maze of tunnels. They were both thrown off the cliff immediately. The next day, when she sat at the cliff's edge, she looked for their bodies but saw nothing, not even bones.

On a trip coming back from the land above, one of the men was carried down the path, bleeding from a wound in his stomach that he had received in a fight with a gambling opponent. She had heard the men report that he had cheated. The wounded man died shortly after, groaning as one of the women tried to stop the bleeding.

Dirty Nose wondered if she would groan or scream as the monsters feasted on her body. Her examination of the land below took on a heightened urgency as she sat on the cliff edge, but day after day, she saw nothing disturbing the placidity of the water.

The leader came and went on many gambling expeditions, but she dared not speak to him about her fate. She thought that perhaps he did not realize that she knew of his plans.

When he kicked her just before he went on his latest mission, she winced but said nothing. She hoped that he would never see the monsters in the water, but then, if he did not, would he give her to the men as their plaything? She shuddered, and went back to her duties, carrying slop to the cliff's edge and throwing it to the rocks below.

She was sleeping when the leader and his men returned, dragging a slave behind them. They yelled as they came down the path and woke everyone with their noise. The leader strutted around the fire and thrust out his chest, pulling the slave behind him, shouting how he had won him from a tribe of giants. The leader had been cunning and had been victorious, especially because he had cheated.

Some of the women went to the slave and pushed him next to the fire so all could see. He was a young man, with long, blond hair and an air of strength about him. Standing in the light of the fire, he frowned at being stared at and stood very straight until a woman kicked one of his legs. He stumbled, and then Dirty Nose could see that his left leg was crooked. She could see scars below his knee.

He recovered from the kick, and, as he did, he limped, favoring his leg. The woman who had kicked him screamed and laughed and pointed at his leg.

"Limp!" she cried. "He limps!"

"Limp! Limp! Limp!" the women shouted, laughing as they poked him.

They soon got tired of him and shoved him away from the fire. He stumbled into the dark and stopped in front of Dirty Nose. In the darkness, it was difficult to navigate on the granite shelf, and it was clear that he had no idea what to do next.

Dirty Nose reached out to him and said, "Take my hand."

Limp, for that was now his name, complied, and followed the girl as she showed him the cliff edge, warning him not to climb down, and then led him to the caves where he was soon gratefully asleep.

Limp and Dirty Nose became friends as the days passed. They would sit on the edge of the cliff together, looking at the land and water below. She told him of the monsters in the water and her fate to be eaten by them—if it came to that. Limp wanted to confront the leader and defend her, but the girl shook her head.

"No, you cannot. Any slave that causes trouble is thrown off the cliff. They do not care, because it is so easy to get more."

He ground his teeth but agreed.

"We should escape from here," he whispered.

Dirty Nose shook her head. "Some have tried, but they are always caught by the guards as they make their way up the path and through the tunnels. And then they are thrown off the cliff."

Limp looked over the edge. "Why can we not escape this way? We could climb down, I think."

She looked horrified and replied, "But then we would die, eaten by the monsters. They have told many tales of those who went down, never to return."

The young man studied the cliff and the land and water below, and said, "I do not see any monsters."

Dirty Nose shuddered. "They are there. They must be. When they threw a slave to his death, the very next day, his body was gone. Not even bones were left. I am afraid to go that way."

She sighed, sadly, and said, "I think we will grow old and die here. Unless the leader sends me to die below. But I do not want to speak of it anymore."

Limp and Dirty Nose spent their days together after that, as much as they could, between their different chores, so much so that the women noticed, and tittered at the sight of "slave love."

The leader ignored them both, and left on multiple trips, but returned empty-handed and irritable. His luck at gambling had evaporated, and the women of the tribe began to question his abilities. He was convinced that there was a dark sign in the air, and always made sure to scan the water below the cliff as he marched down the path from the lands above.

Dirty Nose was pushing a mound of slop over the edge of the cliff when the men came back from their latest expedition. The leader was bellowing as he ran down the path.

"They have come!" he yelled. "They have come back!"

He stood at the fire and motioned toward the cliff.

"I saw the monsters in the water at the high path on the mountain," he said. "The water is dark with their evil, and they will come for us unless we give them what they want."

Some of the women turned toward the cliff edge to look, but the leader shouted, so loudly that the women next to him covered their ears.

"No! Do not look at them! Never look at them! They will see us and know that we are many. They will not be satisfied with one, and will pursue us until we all have been ripped apart by their teeth."

He collapsed on the granite rock and started rocking back and forth. For all his bravery, he was now a man ruled by panic, for he had seen what they had not.

"Their teeth!" he exclaimed. "Their teeth are larger than all the teeth in the world."

One of his women held him against her breasts and stroked his head, murmuring in his ear. The other women scuttled away from the cliff, stumbling over each other as they did. They would not be the fool-ish ones to bring the monsters swarming into their camp.

Gradually, the leader started to breath more slowly, as his woman held him tightly. He grunted at her and carefully stood up, aware that he had displayed unfortunate weakness in front of the tribe. But as a gam-bler and a skilled trickster, he knew of an easy way to turn their attention away from his failings.

"Dirty Nose!" he bellowed. "Bring me Dirty Nose!"

Dirty Nose tried to hide, but was lifted up by two of the men and carried to the leader, and dropped on the stone without a word.

She glared at the men and nursed her arm that had been scraped. She tried to make herself very small, but it was no good. The leader stood her up and pointed at her, looking at his assembled followers.

"This slave will quench the monsters' hunger, and our good fortune will return."

The men and women of the tribe laughed, relieved that they would not be devoured, and started to dance around Dirty Nose, hurling insults and grim tidings quite ungratefully.

"Dirty Nose is a meal for many! Dirty Nose ripped limb from limb! Dirty Nose with no nose left! No bones, no skin, no fat, no muscle! Dirty Nose to the monsters!"

Their songs and shouts were interrupted by Limp, who strode up to the leader and loudly proclaimed, "No! I will go in her place!"

The leader was taken aback since slaves were not supposed to do anything other than live as slaves and exhaust themselves at their tasks. His mouth opened and shut more than once before he laughed, and said, "I will send you both to the monsters."

Limp shook his head and replied, "No. If you do, they will know that we are many and will come for us all. If you send only me, they will have their meal and depart. I am bigger than the girl, and will satisfy them well."

The leader stared at Limp and then looked at the other members of the tribe and the assembled slaves. It seemed that he was counting and weighing things as if he were throwing bones in a game. After a moment, he nodded and declared, "Yes! This slave will fill the monsters' bellies more than the girl. He will do!"

Without a pause, he and his men took Limp by the arms and walked toward the cliff, taking care to not get too close. The leader looked at

Limp and pointed toward the edge. "Go! Go down the cliff to the monsters. If you do not, we will send the girl."

Limp turned and gazed at Dirty Nose and smiled. His long, blond hair was filthy from his work, and his face and nose were dirty too. But his eyes were warm and filled with light as he looked at the girl. Without a word, he lowered himself over the cliff and disappeared from view.

Dirty Nose screamed and sobbed and was going to run to the cliff to follow him, but the women held her back and scolded her.

"We cannot let the monsters know that we are many."

She hit at them and cried, but they held her until she grew calm. They finally let her go and went back to their cooking. The men had brought new birds to roast, and they were hungry.

₦ ₦ ₦

Limp was a few feet below the edge, standing on a small outcrop of rock, looking for the best way to climb down. He heard Dirty Nose crying, and closed his eyes for a moment, breathing heavily. He had not thought it would come to this.

When he opened his eyes, he saw his way, and slowly moved down the cliff, from rocky point to root to crack to edge to rocky point. He was so concentrated on his work that he was quite surprised to find himself standing on the sand. He had made it, just as night began to fall. The moon was full that night, which fortunately gave him light to creep across the sand toward the water.

He moved slowly, peering at the water nervously. He was on a strip of sand with trees on his left and the water on his right. He had never seen anything like it. It kept coming toward the sand as if it were alive, and then, just before it reached the sand, it would dissolve with a splash into whiteness. He dipped his fingers in it and put them in his mouth and then spat. It wasn't like the water of the river where he had grown up, swimming and fishing with his brothers. They could drink that water, but this new type of liquid had a sharp taste that he couldn't identify.

He kept looking for movement in the water and the dark shapes of monsters. As he crept forward, sometimes standing, sometimes on his hands and knees, he tried to reconcile the awful fact that he would soon be ripped apart and eaten.

As the moon broke out from behind a cloud, he saw them.

There were long, roiling shapes in the water, some rushing toward him and circling around, while others simply floated, waiting for him to arrive. As he stared at them, he realized that he could run. He did not have to be eaten. He could run down the sand, past the monsters, and be gone before the moon went behind another cloud. He stood up and started to walk along the sand, as far away from the water as he could, when the terrible thought came to him that if he ran, the monsters would turn their attention to the cliff and to the tribe, and most of all to Dirty Nose.

He wanted to cry at that thought, but simply shook his head fiercely, and wiped his eyes and continued walking toward the monsters. As he got closer, he paused, and dropped to his stomach, pressing himself against the sand. There was something strange in front of him, lying at the edge of the water.

It was a monster, with half of its horrible body in the water and half on the sand. As the moon came out, he could see it more clearly. It was not dark-colored at all, but rather a shade of gray like the granite of the encampment. His dread of being eaten was now tinged with curiosity. Perhaps the monster was dead!

He crept forward, on his hands and knees, until he was directly in front of the monster. It was breathing slowly, and its eye was looking at him. It had a cavernous mouth and an eye on each side of its head. It had no arms with claws like most monsters. Instead, it had what looked like wings on each side of its body. Its mouth was partially open, and he could see its teeth. They were rather small, and he was perplexed that there was no blood dripping from them.

He crouched in front of the monster, studying it. He could see the other monsters in the water, swimming back and forth, some frantically. Some of them were screaming and whistling in a frightful way. The beast in front of him wasn't making any sound at all, except for the sound of its breath.

There was a mystery about the monster that gnawed at his thoughts, a sense of familiarity that he couldn't understand. He was thinking so hard that he inadvertently pounded his forehead and then fell backward onto the sand in shock. Something had touched his shoulder.

He turned, crouching, ready to fight a new monster, to die without tears or fear, and then sat down with a gasp. It was Dirty Nose, standing over him, smiling.

"No one was watching me, so I crept away and followed you down the cliff."

Limp opened his mouth and shut it again and then stood up and, with one large stride, scooped up Dirty Nose in his arms and hugged her. She giggled and hugged him tightly in return.

After a moment, she pointed at the monster on the sand and said, "I do not think it is a monster."

He carefully put her down and turned and looked, and finally understood what his mind had been trying to get through to him.

He looked at Dirty Nose and said, "It is like a fish! I kept thinking that it seemed like a fish. But not exactly like a fish."

Dirty Nose looked up at him. "What is a fish?"

Limp thought for a moment, and said, "It is like a bird, but it swims in water."

"Oh," she said.

She didn't feel afraid of it, for some reason, so she walked up to it and put her hand on its nose. She ran her hand along its snout and then bent down and looked at its eye. After a moment, she sat and placed her forehead against its head between its eyes. It seemed to Limp that she was listening.

She stood up and looked at him and said, "It wants to go back in the water. If it does not go in the water, it will die."

Limp looked at the monster that was not a monster and not a fish, and went up to it and looked at its eye. The creature looked at him and then let out a very tiny whistle. It was an exhausted, on-the-point-of-death whistle, and it reached into Limp's heart and pulled at it.

He looked at Dirty Nose, and then, without a word, they started to push the monster into the water. It was slow going because the fish-creature was very heavy. After struggling to push it, they decided to lift it and pull it, one pull at a time. Dirty Nose was stronger than Limp had thought and managed to raise the monster just enough for Limp to pull and coax it toward the water.

The monsters in the water were whistling as they worked, but their whistles sounded different and less frantic. The moon went in and out of the clouds many times, observing their labors, until finally, with a great splash, the monster's massive body was submerged in the water. It looked at Limp and Dirty Nose, and rolled over and over in the water, splashing its tail, and just before it turned away, it whistled, a beautiful, piercing whistle that said, "I am alive, and thank you."

At least that is what they thought it meant.

The monster swam out to the others, and, in a flash, they were all gone, bobbing and weaving and jumping as they swam away from the shore.

Limp and Dirty Nose were exhausted and sat on the sand, watching them go. She put her hand in his and placed her cheek against his shoulder.

"I am glad that we were not eaten by monsters."

Limp laughed and agreed. "Yes! I also did not want that."

They sat for a while, and then Dirty Nose jumped up. She tugged on his hand until he stood up.

"We have to scream and yell as loudly as we can so that the leader will think that we are being eaten. I am sure that they are listening."

Limp looked toward the cliff. "Do you think they are looking, too?"

"No," she said. "They do not want the monsters to see them. They will be afraid because I am also gone, but they will hear us and think that we are dead, and then we will not have to go back."

He looked at her and grinned. "We do not have to go back!"

She laughed and nodded, and then they screamed—horrific screams of bloody carnage and limbs ripped and stomachs gouged. They ran wildly up and down the sand, waving their arms crazily and screaming until they both stopped and let out one gigantic scream.

They listened carefully for a moment and heard the tribe shouting and laughing. They could imagine the leader grandly puffing out his enormous stomach and announcing that he knew it would work all along.

Limp took her hand in his, and they turned away from the cliff and walked along the sand. The moon was still lighting their way, and they could see a meadow at the far end of the sand.

They quickened their pace, and Limp looked at Dirty Nose, and asked, "You know that Limp is not my name?"

She gazed up at him fondly and squeezed his hand. "Dirty Nose is not mine."

They walked for a moment in silence.

"What is your real name?" he asked.

She smiled shyly and said, "My mother always called me Flower."

She put her arm around his waist and asked, "What is your name?"

He looked abashed and said, "Lion."

He looked at his leg, with its scars, and said, "But now it is Broken Lion."

She stopped and touched his leg and then stood on her toes and kissed him. They suddenly realized that they had never kissed. It was fascinating, so they kissed some more.

Catching her breath, she started to walk again, holding his hand.

Looking up at him, with her face bright under the moonlight, she said, "I will just call you Lion."

He smiled down at her and kissed her again. He pointed at the meadow, and then at the sea.

"I will teach you how to swim, and to bathe, and you will show me how to cook."

Flower just sighed and smiled, and squeezed his hand tightly. She was very, very happy, but she was always curious, so she asked, "What does it mean, to swim, and to bathe?"

Lion lifted her in his arms and walked into the water, and gently lowered her so that only her face was above the water. She had never been in water, and if it were not for Lion's strong arms, she would have struggled. But he was gentle, and his eyes gleamed as he smiled, so she relaxed and felt soothed by the water.

He dipped his hand in the water and rubbed her face gently and washed the smudges off her nose. Her face had a lifetime of dirt embedded in it, but there was some improvement as he stroked her face.

He smiled at her as she floated in his arms under the moon. He kissed her and said, "No one will ever call you Dirty Nose again."

Flower was extremely pleased to hear that, and looked up at Lion, resting in his arms and thinking. She wasn't quite sure what to say but decided on the very best thing she could imagine.

She smiled—a wide, glorious, bursting smile—and asked, "Can you kiss me again?"

He did, and she kissed him in return. After quite a long time, they stood, and she pointed at the meadow and laughed.

"Dear Lion, can you catch me?"

She ran toward the meadow, slowly so that he could keep up with his limp, and just as they reached the grass, she stopped and took his hand. She had no memory of grass and stared at it perplexed.

Lion picked her up and carried her onto the grass, and then continued walking. He carried her deeper into the meadow until they could no longer hear the waves slapping against the sand.

The beach behind them was empty. The whistling monsters were nowhere to be seen, and the leader and his band on the plateau were finally asleep.

Lion stopped, and Flower slid from his arms and stood next to him. They had reached a grove of trees next to a wide pool of water. The night wind was rustling the leaves of the trees, and the fields around them were quiet.

Flower gazed at the pond in front of them, and at the meadow, and the moon resting just above the trees. She looked up at Lion and pressed her body against him. With the threat of monsters behind them, she felt, for the first time in her life, that she might be able to relax.

But she wasn't sure. The fields and trees in front of them seemed vast to her, and as she stared at them, and the shadows of the night, she felt afraid again. What dangers were sliding between the trees? Would they be discovered by the leader as he roamed the land looking for slaves?

She shook her head in anger. She would never go back. She would rather die. Her breathing grew louder, and her body tensed against Lion's side, and her hands curled tightly into fists.

And then she felt Lion's hand on her cheek, caressing her softly. She looked up at him and saw him smiling at her. He drew her closer to him, and lifted her chin, and said the one thing that she needed to hear, the one thing that shielded her from the terrors of the night. Her body trembled in relief as he gazed down at her and spoke with a voice that banished her fears entirely.

"May I kiss you again?"

The Last Person

It was the expression on the woman's face that had caught the monk's attention. It was one of those quiet, inscrutable expressions that gnawed at one's mind, begging to be understood, yet at the same time running in full retreat from the cruelty of gawkers.

The monk had sat for a long time, staring at the harsh black and white photograph of the East Indian woman and her child, trying to quiet his mind and reach into the woman's eyes that gazed down at the ground with utter resignation. The child pressed against her shoulder was frenzied, mouth wide with a cry of hurt and confusion, eyes bewildered with tears. Her left hand held him, fingers wrapped in his hair, while she leaned into her other hand with weary desperation.

The monk had studied the photo intently that day in the library, wondering which conflict had provided the wartime photographer with his involuntary subjects. The monk had a certain distaste for the frequent callousness of photographers who caught humanity in the midst of agony. He had often thought that they should throw their cameras down and pick up the victims instead. Yet on that day, he was grateful that the photographer had clicked his shutter when he did.

In the days after the monk had visited the library, he had been unable to shake the haunting pain of the woman's eyes—which was odd, really, since the shadows in the photograph had all but obscured her eyes, leaving only black pools of sadness. Her eyes followed him as he made his rounds, stumping his way through the hot Nevada sun, brushing the sweat off his forehead in irritation.

Nevada had been hard on the monk. He had been thrilled to climb over the stony parapets in the desert, to sit baking on the granite while the air taunted him, bringing no relief. He hadn't minded the heat in the desert, because he had been utterly enthralled with the idea that the stones he sat upon were contemporaries of humankind's history. It was the lack of grass that had helped him sense the absolute age of the rocks around him, an age that stretched all the way back to the first ancestors of humankind. The starkness of the scene had hit him suddenly as if it was a mute witness to thousands of years of tears and bloodshed.

The monk could see why the old biblical prophets had been able to maintain their fervor in the desert. The atmosphere seemed to resonate with the feeling that God was present, and had been present throughout all the long years of war and attrition, silent and lonely and suffering.

It wasn't the desert that clawed at the monk's soul, making him feel as if his skin was being ripped away while he helplessly watched. It was Nevada's other side, the seamy underbelly of a beast that flaunted its bravado on billboards and in neon lights, at crap tables and on stages crowded with soulless dancers who beckoned to middle-aged men.

The monk had fought against the city's seduction, gripping his fists, clenching his jaw until his muscles twisted in spasm. He had come to discover that the strength of will by itself was failing him, leaving him weakened, twisting, clutched by the spiritual glue that crept along the night streets of Las Vegas and Reno.

His superior had tried to help him one day, kindly explaining that spiritual laws were only useful as long as one wanted to follow them—and that one day he might simply decide to throw his vows and regulations in the trash. The monk had gulped a bit but hadn't really understood.

Until now. He finally understood how utterly useless the law was in the face of overwhelming human desire. The cloying, winking sensuality of Las Vegas had beaten at the monk's physical desires for so long that he no longer felt the power of moral restrictions. It wasn't that he believed that restraint was wrong. He knew, from the top of his youthful head all the way to his sore feet, that he was a prisoner of his religious code. There was no escape for the monk, for he found it impossible to deny his belief that a life of purity was the best way to find happiness.

His problem was that he no longer cared if he was condemned. In fact, he was convinced that he would indeed be miserable if he finally cast his vows aside. His dark imaginings vividly created his future torment, an icy hell shut away in mud and gloom.

It was the brothels that had tipped the scales toward perdition for the monk. He had stepped through their portals as he meandered through his faithful errands and had stood his ground against an onslaught of desire. Matters were worsened when he discovered that women of the night seemed rather nice—even polite. Surprisingly, they respected him and told each other not to tempt him, for he was, after all, a nice boy of the church. He had stumbled away, unscathed in virtue, but poisoned by a vapor that clung and didn't wash off.

Surrounded by his friends, who seemed flawless to him, and more faithful, the monk had grimly maintained a façade of normalcy. He was grateful for the company of faith, for it was more difficult to run screaming toward the gates of hell when one's friends were standing guard. It was thus that the monk greeted the news of his pioneer mission with a fear that sickened him. As an exercise of faith, he was to go to the northern city of Reno for forty days—without money, without lodging, and, worst of all, without a soul to protect him from himself.

As he trudged through his first days in Reno, the monk's trepidation was confirmed. The loneliness of being confronted with his own pock-marked soul was overwhelming. There was no escape from his self-examination—no crowd of friendly faces to distract him from the reality that his mind and faith were collapsing under the stress of a ruthless physical desire.

The monk wandered, with no ability to work or spread the word. Because he was hungry and didn't want to sleep outside, he forced himself to ask for donations in store parking lots. As soon as he had enough money for a room and his daily meals, he would stop, too depressed to do more.

He took to walking the streets, blindly pushing himself along without caring where he was going, without noticing where he ended up. He found a self-service laundromat that was warm and hospitable, a place where he could be ignored as he sat and stared at nothing in particular.

Hours passed, and housewives glanced at him curiously. He was too dull to care and buried his head even farther into the collar of his jacket. It was hunger that finally drove him to stand up and creakily walk out into the empty streets.

Night had fallen, and the streetlights were no help at all to his bitter mood. Their light threw a blue sheen against the pavement as he marched defiantly, block after block. He had reached the conclusion that the suffering of hell was no longer a deterrent to his overwhelming desire. It seemed a reasonable bargain to the monk to trade eternal suffering in the distant future for a raucous life of pleasure in the present. The threat of punishment and the fear of hell no longer had the power to spur the monk toward a life of endless religious sacrifice. He began to wonder where he might go after casting off the trappings of religion. It occurred to him that he might find employment in a brothel. At least then, he could enjoy himself before he died and was pulled into hell.

As the monk passed house after house of sleeping occupants, his mood grew perverse, and he idly considered throwing himself in front of a passing car, thus ending his dilemma. He began to calculate, rather sullenly, the number of people who might grieve at his untimely death. At first, he was sure that no one would miss him. No one would care. He knew it was true, for he was in a black mood without a trace of light.

His self-pity deepened, and he began to think of all the people whom he knew, wondering in turn if they would be saddened by his passing, whether by fatal accident or by his descent into a life of hedonistic pleasure. The monk knew many people and, being a reasonably sociable person, had developed numerous friendships in his years of service. He hesitated, as he mentally skipped from person to person, questioning whether or not they cared about his miserable existence.

His hesitation deepened as he continued, and he began to wonder if perhaps his friends might care about him after all. The night grew colder, and he shivered as he buttoned up his thin jacket. The idea that his friends might be saddened by his spiritual or physical demise began to take root in his heart, as he walked more and more slowly past the darkened houses. The monk began to worry about his friends' reactions, and it occurred to him that they might feel grief when he was gone.

It was the knowledge that they would grieve that turned him. He glanced at his reflection in the windows of cars that were already beginning to glisten with early morning dew. His face was pale and distraught, and he was startled by his look of exhaustion.

The street that he was walking on reached an intersection, and the monk aimlessly wandered into a parking lot, where he sat and gazed at the mist moving across the shop lights. The monk was faintly surprised to find himself thinking about his friends and their feelings. He had been reveling in his own misery for so long that he found it strange to consider anyone else.

The barren tint of the streetlights began to remind the monk of his epiphany in the desert. He had come away from his trek over the rocks with the conviction that God had endured a history of loneliness. As he sat shivering on the curb of the parking lot, with his chin in his hands, his sense of devastation was assuaged by the realization that his own loneliness was tiny compared to the heart of an abandoned God.

Impervious to the roar of a caravan of trucks that barreled through the intersection, the monk finally crumpled, overwhelmed with sadness that he had forgotten God. He couldn't stand the thought that God was lonely and began to feel stirrings of a deep and abiding sympathy.

As dawn streaked across the parking lot, bringing with it a clatter of delivery trucks, the monk rose stiffly and blinked rapidly. He felt thoroughly exhausted but simultaneously refreshed in an unexpected way. He smiled at a young mother walking toward him, with three children in tow. He was delighted when she smiled back at him.

The monk rubbed his unshaven chin ruefully and wondered if people would find his rumpled appearance amusing. He spied a doughnut shop in the far distance and began to trudge toward it, anticipating with some eagerness the aroma of hot coffee.

He smiled at people on the sidewalk as he passed them, hoping that he could brighten their day just a tiny bit. The monk liked people and was beginning to remember how much he enjoyed serving them. He had spent many hours meeting people in their neighborhoods and had always been touched by people's reactions when he was able to care for their needs.

People were streaming by on the sidewalk, and traffic was getting heavier as the sun rose higher in the sky. The monk began to wonder how many people he might touch with service or love during the rest of his life. He started to calculate how many years he would be alive, and how many people he would meet during those years. His stomach was growling by this time, complaining in a very undignified way about its neglect. Its loud digestive rumblings jogged the monk's thoughts, and he started to wonder what would happen to the people he was destined to meet if he turned away from a life of service.

In his reverie, the monk almost stumbled over a rock on the sidewalk. Looking up sheepishly, he saw that he had arrived at the front door of the doughnut shop. He swung open the door and quietly sat down at the counter. Gazing around at the customers busily munching on pastries thick with cream and chocolate, he came to the quiet conclusion that hell could only be avoided when one wanted to avoid hell for the sake of others. He would either be there for people, or he would pass them by. Biting into his doughnut, he knew that he couldn't ignore their suffering.

The next day, the monk was surrounded by a stack of books in the Reno public library. The transformation in his heart felt very powerful, but he was worried about his immature heart and internal conflict. He was grimly certain that his body's desires would prove recalcitrant and would never easily surrender. He didn't know exactly what he was searching for, but he wanted to find something that would help him remember the suffering of the people who would need his love in the future. The monk was convinced that his victory depended upon his desire to care for others.

He thought it might have been God who guided him to find the photograph of the woman and her child. He was astonished when he saw it, for the woman's face seemed to reflect all that he had gone through the night before. He looked at her sorrowful eyes and knew that someday in the future, a woman like her, with a child at her side, would need him. Not because he had anything particularly special to give to her, but simply because he would be there when the time came.

The monk carefully copied the photograph that day, and later replaced it with an original page from a copy of the book that he purchased at a store. He carried the photograph with him in his travels and placed it where he could see it frequently. He didn't know if the woman was alive or dead but secretly hoped that he would meet her someday. She had come to represent more than her own misfortune, in the monk's eyes. He had begun to see her as a symbol of the person at the farthest corners of the earth, the last person to be liberated from suffering. The woman's grief had given the monk the treasure of simplicity, the awareness that he could never rest if there was pain still left in the world.

The Orchid Queen

Can an orchid forget?

One might not think so, but this one forgot. She was born next to a thicket of vines in a forest that echoed with the thrum of bullets and the animosity of men. When she was very young, a boot had fallen on her body, exhausting her in a bewilderment of panic as she struggled to free herself. Eventually, the boot had been dragged away, leaving behind scars and confusion in her delicate heart.

It was not simply that she was ignored by the soldiers marching on the path next to her home. She might have endured that, taking comfort in the admiration of animals and birds. Her tears—for orchids can indeed shed tears—grew from a profound sense of violation and pain. The foul acridity of tobacco juice often marred the ground around her, splashing across her flowers as she cringed in revulsion. More than one soldier stopped to urinate, unaware that she was choking from the fumes.

Each year should have brought pride in the new growth of her leaves and petals. Instead, she was filled with unease as the forest trembled with the sounds of war. Bodies fell across the path, slamming into the earth with terrifying thuds. Her serenity was so disturbed by the continued years of conflict that she began to droop, even forgetting how to breathe. Sometimes she wondered if she had gone mad.

She had not gone mad. She had fallen prey to the pain of loneliness and the sorrow of a violent world. Her heart had become so troubled that she no longer remembered that she was an orchid. Surrounded as she was by the smoke and noise of a world out of touch with beauty, her loss of identity was complete.

Hopeless, she pressed her body against the earth and prepared to die.

Fortunately for her, dying can be a slow and uncooperative process. She didn't die, which vexed her greatly. Being stubborn, as some orchids tend to be, she continued to rest her body on the rich, dark earth, wondering idly how long it would take for death to come.

Her emotions had been so damaged that she found it difficult to rest. Her mind was turbulent, and her thoughts returned again and again to the boot that had crushed her and the pain and resentment that had overwhelmed her soul. She hated the men who had filled her home with foulness and noise and continuous warfare. If an orchid could shriek, her cries would have been terrifying.

Since she could not shriek, she lay against the earth in silence. Her breathing grew slower, and the erratic pulses of energy shooting along her stem began to gradually respond to a rhythm that she had forgotten. The earth, the moist, life-giving soil on which she lay, had its own pulse that played against her, caressing her petals, coaxing her to listen.

Having nothing better to do, she pressed herself deeper into the earth and examined the cadence of the world around her. She had not noticed such things for a very long time. Her pain had created impenetrable walls around her, condemning her to an unnecessary prison. Now, as she listened, she heard the gentle steps of animals walking along the forest paths. She heard the music of her friends the birds and felt the whispered breathing of other plant life.

The earth beneath her was so warm and so embracing that she was sure that she felt the energy of the entire world swirling into her delicate roots and body. The energy was exuberant and made her feel lightheaded and frothy. She shifted one of her petals and glanced up at the sky and noticed with some surprise that the sun was bathing her body. She had forgotten how delightful the sun could be.

She was fascinated by the interplay of the sun with the leaves of the trees above her and began to feel slightly hypnotized as she watched. The trees seemed to bend toward her, nodding at her and speaking to her with the rustling of their leaves. She lay there quietly, gazing at the details around her. A deer mouse was standing on a rock in front of her and looking at her curiously, chewing on a seed. She ordinarily didn't pay much attention to mice, but this one seemed like a splendid little fellow. He squeaked at her, and she laughed, as orchids sometimes do.

Many hours passed, and she discovered that she had forgotten how to listen. The world of the forest was filled with secret words of love that spoke of oneness and strength and peace. Her senses opened, and she began to feel that her roots were intertwined with every plant and tree, every clump of earth and vein of rock, deeper and deeper, spreading far beyond the forest.

As she listened, her petals began to shine, and the energy coursing from the earth gave her the strength to lift her body from the forest floor. Sunlight washed across her, and as it did, she realized that the vibrancy of the hidden world had cleansed her pain and feelings of resentment toward the boot and the filth and the violence of men.

The forest seemed to understand her transformation, and sent warm currents of air across her body, caressing her gently and murmuring her name in approval, which brought a flush of pink to her petals. She had forgotten her name. She had forgotten what it meant to be an Orchid Queen, to be a flower that was directly connected to the earth, a flower that gleamed with the resonance of the joy that created her.

As she straightened her body, she curtsied to the trees and the plants and the animals around her and nodded at the white-footed mouse. She whispered a promise to the earth as she curtsied: a promise to never forget who she was, and a promise to never forget to listen to the hidden world.

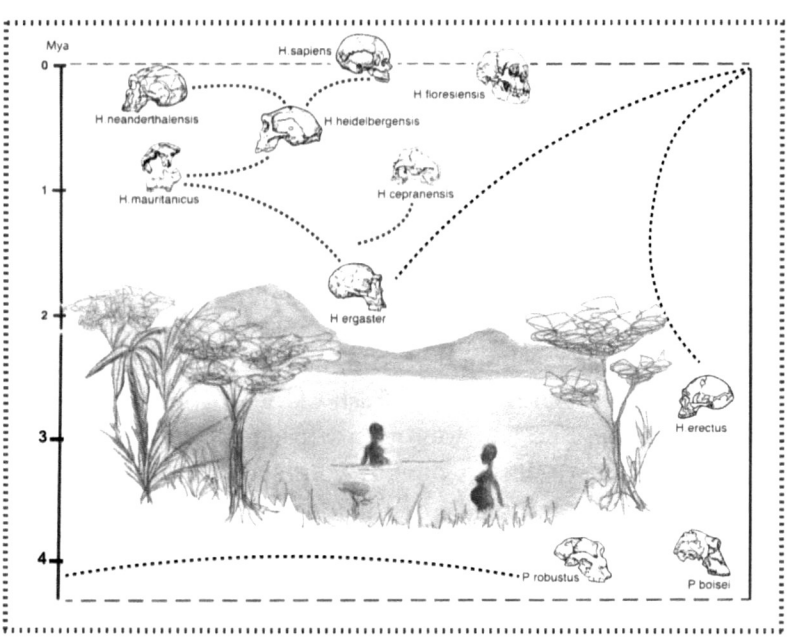

Birth

*B*eing naked, hot, and dirty was normal for the small tribe that lived on the edge of the foothills on the East African plain. The daily struggle and violence of life a million and a half years ago made novelties like bathing entirely unnecessary. Thus, the actions of two of the women in the tribe seemed to the others to be an incomprehensible waste of time. Even the leader of the group, possessed as he was with superior strength and intelligence, gazed in bewilderment whenever the women walked into the river and bathed.

The two women refused to explain why they bathed so frequently. When asked, they simply shrugged. They had both dreamed a mysterious dream—a secret dream. A man as tall as the clouds had pointed at their bellies and smiled. He had lifted them into the sky and carried them on his hand to the river's edge, where he had gently nudged them into the water and shown them how to bathe. After waking from their dream, they had made their first tentative forays into the river, not knowing what to expect. They had been surprised by the pleasure they felt as the cool water washed away their sweat and grime. They liked the experience of being clean.

They had known each other all their lives, but it wasn't until they found themselves in the river, day after day, that they realized they were friends. When they compared the growing size of their bellies, they glanced at their mates, hunkered over a freshly killed animal with the other men, and then looked at each other and laughed as they sank back into the river and floated luxuriously on their backs.

The other women had borne many children but had never resorted to games like floating in rivers. Most of them had gone about their duties and delivered their children without much thought. Biting off their children's umbilical cords were minor incidents that caused hardly a flicker of interest from their hunter mates.

The two women, and their habit of bathing in the river, gradually caused more and more consternation within the group. Their skin had become shiny and clean—an unusual state for members of the Ergaster tribe. As the weeks and months passed, and their bellies grew, the women grew stubborn and refused to work in the hottest part of the day. The elder of the two women had an especially difficult time with her mate and argued loudly when he pushed her to sharpen his stone blade. Instinctively, she knew that she had to rest and preserve the child growing inside her.

The younger woman had a much easier experience, perhaps because her mate was intensely curious about her condition. He continually passed his fingers across her swollen belly, marveling at the shape as it expanded. Neither of the women had ever borne a child before, and they were increasingly nervous as the day of delivery drew near. They had shown their bellies to some of the older women, who had patted them and grunted approvingly. Their elders' lack of concern had comforted the two younger women to some degree.

When the leader of the group urged everyone to move to some nearby foothills, the two women successfully pleaded with him to stay near the river as they traveled. It was a small victory, easily won, because the leader by this time had begun to view the women as valuable to the tribe. The leader even managed to convince the older women that the "Clean Women," as they had become known, were good luck, and had been the cause of the tribe's successful hunting.

The foothills were a pleasant change after the acrid heat of the plains. The tribe had carried a litter of meat with them and feasted on it hungrily, laughing and shouting to each other about their exploits and plans for the next hunt. The men hardly noticed when the Clean Women went into labor one evening. The older women shooed the men away and kept the two women company as they prepared for birth. The wise women found it fascinating that both women were in labor at the same time. No one could explain why it had happened, but the discussion kept them occupied while they waited through the night. The mothers' contractions lasted for many hours, until, exhausted and bleeding, the two women finally gave birth.

Morning brought with it a long series of amazed exclamations as the men gathered in a circle around the two mothers and their new babies. The elder mother had given birth to a male, while the younger mother was curled up next to her admiring mate, clutching to her breast a tiny baby girl. The leader of the group pushed his way past the other men and pointed at the faces of the boy and girl, scowling at their delicate features. They seemed much too fragile to the leader, with bones that were too small and faces that were too thin. He immediately announced that they wouldn't survive. The older women glared at him, but many of them secretly agreed with the leader. The Homo Ergaster lifestyle was not a suitable one for weak children.

The Clean Women spent the next two years nursing and bathing the boy and girl, drawing unbelieving snorts from the men when they washed the children in the river. The women's breasts, at first heavy with milk, grew smaller as they gradually weaned the boy and girl, feeding them with bits of food that the mothers had carefully chewed in advance. In what seemed to the older women to be surprising good fortune, the babies didn't die that first year, or the second. Instead, they grew healthier and noisier each day. By the end of the second year, the boy and girl had won the grudging approval of everyone in the tribe, including the leader, who had taken to rolling on his back and lifting them in the air above his chest.

The two women walked proudly among the other women, showing off their children, aware that they were indeed exceptional. They had a hard time harnessing the boy and often had to chase him around the camp, followed by a group of screaming and laughing children. The boy spent most of his time attempting to climb the gnarly trees that surrounded their camp. Since he was still so small, he was unsuccessful, but he never stopped trying. His father watched gleefully, laughing when the boy kicked the trees in frustration. Ergaster children were not encouraged to be timid, since weakness and fear often brought an early death.

The boy's boldness was so pronounced that the older men started to murmur that the boy would one day become the leader.

It was the girl, however, who won the hearts of the men and women of the tribe. Even though she displayed the same predilection for bathing as her mother, her sweetness and the warmth of her smile turned even the fiercest, broken-boned old hunters into small children again. If the hunters came back to the camp with bruises or wounds, she would run and examine them with her tiny hands. She filled broken bird eggs with water from the river and poured it over the hunters' cuts. Her tenderness brought the hunters endless amusement since they usually ignored their wounds after they had stopped bleeding. Yet, the girl insisted on wrapping their cuts with bits of grass and even tried crushing flowers into their wounds, causing the men to laugh so hard that one hunter almost choked to death on a bone.

One particular afternoon, just as the sun had started its slow glide toward the foothills, the mothers were talking quietly, watching the boy and girl tumble around their feet. They heard a clamor from some of the men and looked up to see something that none of the Ergaster had ever seen before.

An unusually tall man stood in front of the two mothers, gazing at the boy and girl. None of the members of the tribe had seen him approach, which was very troubling to them since they always kept a close watch for lurking animals around the camp. The leader ran up to the man, asking the man where he had come from. The man smiled and nodded and pointed to the foothills. The leader asked him who he was, and what tribe he came from. He replied with strange words that the leader didn't understand.

Suddenly the man bent down and gently laid his hands on the heads of the two mothers. They were trembling and had scooped their children to their breasts, but they began to feel calmer as he smiled at them. When he pointed at their bellies and laughed, they drew back again in fear. They had forgotten their dream of the man as tall as the clouds. He now stood before them, smiling, whispering to them softly, as they usually did when their children came to them in tears.

He sat down in front of them and massaged their hands gently. He didn't look at all like the Ergaster, and the women silently noted to themselves that, unlike the other men in the tribe, he was extraordinarily clean. The man held out his hands for the boy and girl, and, without knowing why the two women carefully handed the children to him. He cradled them in his arms, enveloping them within his large frame. The toddlers seemed particularly interested in his long, shiny hair. He teased the boy and girl, brushing his hair against their faces until they giggled.

As he played with the children, he started to sing, softly at first, and then very powerfully. The Ergaster loved to sing and had a song for almost every occasion, but the stranger's intricate melodies were startling and immensely attractive to them. Soon the entire tribe was seated around the two women, weaving back and forth as the tall man sang with words and tones that they had never heard. The oldest woman of the tribe, who knew many things, began to weep. She sat next to the stranger and placed her cheek against his shoulder. He smiled at her and continued to sing.

He sang for a long time, caressing the tribe and the women with his voice, leading them through feelings that were unexplainable. The two women leaned against each other, with their arms linked and their eyes unseeing. The stranger's voice had led them back to their dream two years before, back to the end of their vision that they had not understood.

Now, as he sang, they saw their dream again. They saw the stranger grow taller, so large that he once again picked them up and carried them in the palm of his hand. They heard his voice in their minds while they dreamed, if it was a dream, for they also heard him singing, sitting in front of them with their children on his lap.

They watched from the palm of his hand as he strode to the top of a mountain, and then turned his body so that they could see the plains below. If they had not been dreaming, they would have fallen from his hand in fear because of the vastness of the world. As it was, they trembled and shrank back until his singing soothed them. His song brought images and thoughts to their minds, images of an enormous and bewildering world, and thoughts of the One who made everything.

They felt confused in their dream, but the images kept coming, visions of a special light shimmering inside their children, and pictures of their children growing and becoming the leaders of a new tribe who lived with the One who made everything and understood his thoughts. The images were overwhelming to the two women, and they felt relieved as the man stretched out his arm toward their camp. As his hand hovered over the tribe, they were surprised to see themselves, surrounded by a crowd of children, laughing and splashing in the river.

As their vision ended, they saw the tall man sitting silently in front of them, gazing at them with a curious warmth that the women had never seen before. They smiled at him, and he smiled in return. The man slowly stood up, with the children in his arms, and looked around at the tribe, and then at the two women. He spoke, but no one could tell if they heard his words, or just felt them in their minds. He smiled again and said, "You have done very well. You will have many, many children."

The mothers sprang to their feet instinctively, arms outstretched toward their children, with sudden and uncontrollable tears streaming from their eyes. The girl and boy started to cry as the mothers kissed their cheeks passionately, holding their hands and caressing their faces. Finally, the man bent over and carefully and slowly kissed each woman's forehead. His kisses quieted the two women in spite of themselves, and they watched in resignation as the tall man turned and walked rapidly toward the foothills, bearing the children in his arms. The men of the camp, including the two fathers, started to run after the stranger, but the old wise-woman sharply called them back. They reluctantly returned, confused but obedient to the woman's authority.

The leader and the group talked for hours after that, trying to console the two mothers. The entire tribe was in shock. No one could quite agree on why the tall man had come for the children. The wise woman insisted that the Clean Women had done something special. The leader agreed with her and tried to comfort the tribe by making an impromptu speech and declaring that the Clean Women would bring good hunting. He wasn't sure what it all meant, but he encouraged the two women to go into the river and bathe, assuming that the water might help them.

The two mothers sat by the river's edge, blinded by their grief, unable to speak. They rejected their food that evening until the wise woman shook them and forced them to eat. It wasn't until they fell asleep that they found solace. The tall man appeared to them again, smiling and caressing their cheeks and hugging them tightly. They had the same dream for the next two nights, and by the morning of the fourth day, they were able to talk to each other about their children. They told the wise woman about their dreams and were grateful when she nodded sympathetically.

They decided to follow the leader's advice and immersed their bodies in the sparkling water of the river. They lay back, floating for a long time, looking at the sky. The leader watched them for a while, and then grunted sadly and went back to the other men. All the women of the tribe came and sat at the river's edge in silence, hoping that their presence would help the two mothers in some small way. The old wise-woman looked at the two young women as they floated in the water and reminded them that the tall man had said they would have many children. They responded halfheartedly, but as they looked at each other, they knew that the old woman was right.

Far beyond the other side of the foothills, the tall man finally slowed his stride as he approached the edge of a lush valley. He had stopped frequently to care for the children but had still managed to travel very quickly over a great distance. He looked down at the boy and girl, now asleep in his arms, and with a smile began to slowly walk down to the bottom of the valley.

The man sang as he walked—a beautiful melody that filled the air around him. As he approached a meadow at the floor of the valley, other voices joined his as he sang, until the sound of the voices moved in waves across the grass and flowers. Other figures walked next to him, gazing admiringly at the boy and girl, exclaiming at the beauty of their faces.

Finally, he stopped and gently placed the sleeping children on a bed of moss at the foot of a large tree. He straightened and raised his arms toward the sky in gratitude. The atmosphere in the valley had become charged and intense, sparkling in the sunlight and radiating with millions of colors. The children stirred, and he looked down at the girl as she woke. The man smiled at her, and ever so gently touched her nose with the end of his finger.

This story is, of course, conjecture.
Did the human race begin with the birth of two children,
known in the English Bible as Adam and Eve?

Were they born from early hominin parents, under
God's supervision, and with God's spiritual and creative input?

Will we ever know what really happened? I hope so . . .

The Attack of
the Devil Bug Gang

They were an ordinary couple living on an unremarkable street on an uneventful day. There were no fire trucks screaming by, no dogs barking in the distance. It was a sleepy Saturday morning, and they were cleaning, and carrying things, and doing their best to be useful.

The night before, they had been quite happy and had spent the evening out of the house, holding hands romantically.

Thus, they were unprepared and utterly unaware of the evil cloud of drooling creatures plummeting toward their home.

But that's the way it is with a Devil Bug Gang.

Members of Devil Bug Gangs are exceptionally smelly creatures, rank with layers of sweat and an atmosphere of curse words not spoken in our parts for a very long time. They are often old and terribly vain and angry. No, they are more than angry. They are cruel and hateful and have but one joy and one goal flickering behind their cesspool eyes.

They fly, for they are far too lazy to walk. They fly in gangs and spit and cackle as they go, searching, ever searching, for their next victims. Their names are long forgotten, even to themselves, so they call each other "Scum" and "Vomit," and if they're feeling particularly gleeful, they sometimes refer to each other as "Putrescence." One of their favorite pastimes, when they're not "working," is reading tabloid newspapers. They absolutely adore yellow journalism, and they do their best to instigate messy events that will end up as headlines. They are especially attracted to cheating spouses and murder.

Their leader is always a murderer most foul, for to be their leader, one must be very, very, very bad—the kind of evil that causes a judge to order an immediate execution. Unfortunately, many members of the Devil Bug Gangs that roam across the surface of the world were hanged by the neck until dead, or boiled in oil, or shot at dawn by indignant burghers who couldn't fathom the depth of their crimes.

It is a sad fact, indeed, that snuffing out the life of a dastard does not end his dastardly deeds. Or hers, for that matter. Yes, the Devil Bug Gangs have many females in their company, although any trace of the warmth of a woman's love is certainly not visible in their rotting faces. Devil Bugs are masters of enticement and spend a great deal of time loitering around electric chairs and other devices of state-sanctioned execution. As the switch is thrown, they zoom to the side of the recently departed and whisper seductive blandishments and offers.

They had an easier time years ago when people were killed with axes and guillotines and were drawn and quartered while still alive. Resentful victims howling under cruel and unusual punishments are much more responsive to being led down the gloomy path to the place that the Devil Bug Gangs call home. But even these modern times offer them recruitment possibilities. They do hate clergymen, though, and they're especially frustrated by the many inconsiderate judges who ignore the death penalty and sentence their potential recruits to life in prison. It offers far too much opportunity for repentance and a general rejection of evil deeds. Nuns and social workers make the members of the Devil Bug Gangs gnash their fangs against their leathery lips. Of course, there are exceptions to every rule, and they loudly approve of allowing the most violent prisoners to live longer, as long as they continue to kill and maim their fellow prisoners or order the deaths of more innocent victims beyond their prison walls. They consider such murders to be training for the glorious moments when the felons can join their gang. They also enjoy watching prisoners kill again.

The gangs often fight among themselves and sometimes attack other roaming bands. It's always a frustrating experience for them since they are already dead and can't be killed twice. They content themselves with thinking of new ways to inflict pain on others and ever more creative ways to destroy hopes and dreams and love. Once every thousand years or so, a member of a Devil Bug Gang begins to grow weary of a life of destruction and tries to escape. Then hell does indeed break loose, for Devil Bugs feel intense resentment toward the happiness of others.

One might wonder why they are called "Bugs." Being incorporeal entities, they can make themselves tiny, if they wish, even smaller than angels dancing on the heads of pins. They especially hate angels, even when the angels are not dancing, so the gangs like to escape their notice. They prefer to shrink themselves down to the size of a bug, like a flea or a gnat. Of course, from their point of view, they look the same, so before they embark on a rampage through a village, they find a mirror and preen and primp for hours. Their vanity is so enormous but so misplaced that they have no idea that their clothes are in tatters, or their hair is oily, or their teeth are decayed into stumps. They believe that they're quite handsome. The women among them follow the latest fashions and nowadays indulge in tattoos and piercings. They really like piercings, especially in terribly uncomfortable places. They dress as immodestly as possible and enjoy it very much when the male members of the Devil Bug Gangs are overcome with desire and chase them across the treetops.

Once the gang members are all gussied up, they spit on the ground, and curse and roar, and beat their chests wildly. Then, with a shriek and a buzz, they go hunting. They fly down peaceful suburban roads looking for couples and families who think they love each other. On the way, they might stop at a house where the family members are fighting or cursing or feeling resentful and inject some additional negativity to help things along. They experience a tingling glee when they find a happy couple, a couple who believes in making others happy too. Devil Bugs know all the weaknesses and cracks that they can slip through to destroy such erroneous thinking. Happy indeed! They spit on such egregious nonsense.

The particular Devil Bug Gang that happened to be flying down the street toward our unfortunate couple that Saturday morning was exceptionally skillful in its ability to cause emotional mayhem. Its members specialized in finding the deepest pain in any heart and then flying into the center of that throbbing nerve. Once inside the body of their victim, they begin to scream loudly and incessantly. Their discordant shrieks are worse than the cries of any banshee and cause an immediate disturbance in their unwitting human prey.

As they passed the house of the couple, the leader's telepathic sense was triggered by a wave of peace emanating from the home. He cringed, and growled in his native tongue, an obscure and ancient one, commanding his followers to swoop to the right. They did so, delighted to oblige His Filthiness, His Nastiness, Carbuncle Spew, for that was their name for him. Well, at least the name that one can repeat in polite company.

The gang shrieked in unison and flew through the walls of the house and down the stairs into the basement, where they found the wife. One of the conveniences of being a dead criminal and joining a Devil Bug Gang is that you don't have to knock on doors. You can fly through the thickest of bank walls, and drool over money and gold and then even fly into bedrooms if you wish. The thought of it does make one shudder, doesn't it?

When the gang found the wife, they circled for a moment and quickly found a bruised synapse hidden deep in her heart. With a chortle, they plunged straight into her chest and proceeded to scream and stomp on her emotional wound with their hobnailed boots and kick her nerves with their pointed steel-tipped shoes. They were quite successful since they had chosen her area of pain very carefully. In less than a minute, she wiped the sweat from her brow and spoke to her husband in a very impatient tone, a tone that didn't reflect at all her abiding affection for her beloved.

"What? What are you worried about now? I already know about the mold in the basement!"

The women of this particular gang took great pleasure in persecuting men. They knew all about the ancient rage of women and spent many an hour keening in resentment, howling about the evils that men had done to them. Thus, they waited expectantly for their chance to magnify the husband's pained reaction to his wife's sharp tone. At a signal from the gang leader, they streamed into the husband's body and did their work so well that he immediately responded to his wife's impatience with outrage and walked away, nursing newly felt hurt and confusion.

As he closed the door to the basement, he called down to his wife in a very aggrieved tone, "You didn't have to speak like that!"

The Devil Bug Gang laughed and danced and applauded each other's skill. The women were especially happy, screaming to the leader, "We've got a turtle-shell man!"

Devil Bugs have many names for the various psychological weaknesses they find in their victims. "Killer rage" is their favorite weakness, followed very closely by what they sometimes refer to as the "turtle shell" syndrome. If attacked enough, some individuals will retreat inside themselves, just like a box turtle being plagued by a Southern hunting dog on a hot summer day. They become depressed that they are being attacked and just sit and mope and feel like hiding under a blanket. In fact, sometimes, they do hide under a blanket, which makes the Devil Bugs bounce off the walls in contemptuous laughter. It is a great paradox that Devil Bugs despise the very weaknesses that they work so hard to stimulate in their victims.

Hoping that this particular husband would find a thick, hot, itchy blanket to hide under, the Devil Bugs continued their work, screaming and cursing and pinching and prodding, determined to entirely erase the disgusting atmosphere of happiness that had been circulating through the house.

The husband walked through the kitchen, followed by his wife. As they entered the dining room, he turned quickly and expressed his hurt feelings to her. The gang would have preferred it if the husband had thrown a plate at the wife's head. Hoping for violence, the leader punched his fist directly into a dangling nerve and scraped his fingernails across the wife's internal wound. It was too much for the wife, and she muttered an apology that didn't make her husband feel better at all. The gang leader winked at one of the women, who smiled sweetly back through her dark brown teeth and kicked the husband as hard as she could.

Soon the wounds of both the husband and wife were bleeding copiously. Anger had blown out the lamps of their minds, and Words were being Exchanged.

"Your tone was mean!" said the husband.

"Your pickiness drives me crazy!" responded the wife.

And so it went, with pain and anger escalating amazingly quickly over absolutely nothing at all until the wife left the room in disgust.

A half-hour passed, with the husband and wife sitting in their lonely rooms, staring at the walls and wondering how and why hell had just entered their home. The gang watched anxiously, massaging the couple's emotional wounds with steel wool and sandpaper all the while, hoping that the Next Level would be reached. The Next Level was their favorite part because it included tasty things like rage and curse words and mutterings of hopelessness. In their experience, it didn't take couples very long to reach the Next Level if the gang did its work well.

Much to the chagrin of the Devil Bug women, the husband did not seek refuge under a blanket but instead stood up and walked upstairs to where the wife sat, rocking back and forth in an old rocking chair. Her face was flushed and unhappy, which pleased the gang immensely. The husband said a few things, and the wife responded with pain, which got the gang members' hopes up. The women stayed with the husband as he went into the bathroom for a moment. They were too busy dancing on the husband's invisible sores to notice that he had breathed deeply and looked at himself in the mirror with one of those quiet looks that contain a whole book of prayers. The gang members tried not to notice such things because they had an extreme aversion to sublime looks of any kind.

Thus, they were completely caught off guard when the husband walked to his wife's chair and put his hands on her shoulders, and said, "I'm sorry, darling."

Oh, how the Devil Bugs gnashed their teeth at this display of niceness. Their gnashing got even louder when the wife apologized too. They jumped up and down in fury as the couple sat together by the window and gradually calmed down and remembered that they loved each other. The Devil Bugs hate such things as forgiveness. Ugh, ugh, and blech! The Devil Bugs were thoroughly revolted.

Nothing, however, prepared the Devil Bugs for what came next. As the husband looked out of the window, he chuckled and said, "Hey, I was thinking. You know how we've talked about how evil spirits come back to earth and plague people? Maybe we should give them a name. Maybe they fly around in gangs like little bugs."

The wife said, "Hmm . . . well, maybe."

The husband said, "Okay, how 'bout Devil Bugs? Nasty little bugs that keep messing with us."

The wife laughed and said, "Bugs, huh? Not a bad name. You want some lemonade?"

You can imagine the desperate howls of the gang as they realized that they had been found out. They swirled around the room in angry confusion as the husband took his wife's hand and replied, "Lemonade sounds great."

Devil Bugs try very hard to operate in secret, and they absolutely hate publicity. If they could shoot ministers on sight, they would. They do such an excellent job of covering their tracks that most people have no idea that their emotional wounds are regularly tortured by the perverse attacks of a Devil Bug Gang. To be recognized for what they are is profoundly upsetting to them.

As the husband and wife kissed each other, and hugged, and carried on quite excessively, the leader of the gang cursed in a long string of foul imprecations that made the rest of the group jealous of his fluency. The Saturday morning sun was shining down on the couple as they gradually regained their strength and peace of mind. One of the women of the gang tugged at the leader's greasy sleeve and pointed. He looked and ground his teeth and spat. He was very fond of spitting, especially when he saw angels. There were many of them in the room, gathered around the couple. They might have been there all along, but he didn't know and really didn't care. The leader hated angels and always tried to ignore them, especially at the beginning of the gang's attacks.

The bugs' invasions were most successful when they caught people by surprise. Since many people's wounds were deep, with layer upon layer of scars and broken nerves and cells scraped raw by life, the gang had dozens of vectors of attack. They had found that only a few people were aware of their existence, and fewer still knew how to defend against them. They took it as a challenge when they found defenses erected against them because they knew that people got tired and stressed and careless. If their attack didn't work on a Tuesday, it might work on a Wednesday.

As it was, today was not their day. The leader glared at one of the angels who was standing behind the husband, gently massaging his scalp. The angel looked at the leader with one of those annoyingly piercing looks that angels are known for, which made the gang leader even angrier. He really despised angels, perhaps because he knew that he had no power over them. He scowled again and yelled an order to his gang members. With a shriek of rage, they streamed out of the open window and barreled down the street, staring to the left and the right, looking for another house to invade.

The angels stayed with the man and woman, massaging their shoulders and singing to them. The couple couldn't hear them but suspected that they might be there. It seemed likely to them that they had received help from an unseen source, support that had once again given them the strength to pull themselves out of a morass of confusion.

They had been attacked many, many times by Devil Bug Gangs and knew that they would be invaded again. They were, after all, a quite ordinary couple living on an unremarkable street. The couple never knew who would be targeted first. Sometimes it was the husband, and sometimes the wife. Sometimes the attacks were so fierce that the couple felt driven to the edge of total defeat. It was in their darkest moments that they had been the most grateful for the assistance of invisible helpers.

Over time, the couple had recognized that their wounds didn't define them. The pain was like a bruised knee that kept getting bumped. A bit of salve, some novocaine of love, and proper care would eventually heal each wound in turn. Until then, they had discovered that the daily maintenance of prayer, and expressions of love and forgiveness, were the best defenses against the broken men and women who had forgotten what love meant, who had forgotten happiness, and had instead decided to fly across the world with a Devil Bug Gang.

The Angel Who Fed the Cat

The man woke suddenly, surprised that it was still dark. He rubbed his head as he glanced at his wife sleeping next to him, wondering if it was his headache that had awakened him. He could see their four children sprawled across the other bed and the floor of the motel room, limbs askew in impossible positions.

His feelings sharpened, and he realized that it wasn't his headache that had disturbed his sleep. He'd had a gnawing worry since that morning that their house lay unprotected and vulnerable. They had driven away, locking the doors, turning on lights, and taking all the usual precautions. He had switched on the television, with the idea that burglars would assume that they were home. It wasn't that their house had very many valuables. Most of the furniture was obtained on the fly at Kmart. It was a small house, a rather ugly one, in fact. Not an attractive target for a discriminating robber.

He sighed and peered at the motel room clock. Two a.m. He snuggled under the covers again, comforted by the warmth of his wife. The clock hummed in the silence. He grimaced as he watched the numbers flip slowly by, monotonously reminding him that he was awake.

Two thirty came and went, and the man sat up again with a scowl. Visions of twelve years of computer work scuttling out the door on a hard disk that wasn't backed up flooded his mind. He sat cross-legged in bed, angry that he hadn't taken the time to do that final backup. Grim scenarios crept through his mind, gripping him with the knowledge that he could never replace over a decade's worth of programming data. If he had been prone to ulcers like his father, his stomach would have been in full rebellion. He looked at his wife. She slept, unworried.

The man rose, decisive. He had to do something, anything, to relieve his mounting anxiety. He quietly picked up the phone, and crossed the room to the bathroom door, gingerly stepping over one of his boys. The light from the bathroom formed a dim pool on the carpet as he strained to see the numbers on the phone. He thought that he sounded a bit too dramatic as he whispered into the phone, asking the operator for the number of the police station near his home.

The woman's voice was loud and utilitarian. "Dispatch. May I help you?"

The conversation was brief and frustrating. It was Friday night, and the town didn't have the budget to pay for patrolmen to drive by the houses of worried citizens who were away on visits. He tried to express his hope that some helpful officer might take the time to drive by and see if his house lay open to the night wind—especially since he was a taxpayer, after all—but the dispatcher was firm. Sympathetic, but by the book.

He placed the handset back on the hook, faintly disgusted at the reality of bureaucratic procedures, and creakily walked back to bed. He felt helpless and frustrated that there was really nothing that he could do to protect his all-important computer data from imminent invasion. What really bothered him was the realization that the data would have no value at all to a burglar. The burglar would never know the impact of his callous deed.

The man sat in the narrow bed, with his leg pressed against his wife's hip, and gazed into the dark. There was nothing for it but to pray. He didn't like asking God for such mundane things as the protection of his house and hard drive, although he and his wife made a practice of praying for the safety of their home and their driving when they went on trips. They had done so as they drove away, with their children squeaking out a chorus of tiny amens. He was sure that God was busy, with far more urgent things to worry about.

He closed his eyes, with more than a bit of apology in his thoughts, and prayed. He wanted to make it a delicate but comprehensive prayer— so he prayed that some of God's helpers might have a small amount of time to protect their family's house. He mentioned angels, and the spirits of good people who had died, and any ancestors who might be about, and even their guardian angels. He closed with the prayer that if their home was burgled, life would go on, and yes, they would endure the loss of twelve years of data. He was aware as he murmured, "Amen," that it all seemed embarrassingly small—and he apologized for worrying so much.

He looked at his wife and children one more time and felt glad that he was with them, and that he loved them. With a sigh, he lay down and brought the blanket up to his neck. He yawned as he closed his eyes. It was all in God's hands.

The clock droned as he drifted into a dreamlike state. He saw their house, their ugly, little, blue house, empty under the night sky, with the neighbors unconscious in their slumber. He suddenly thought he saw a man standing at the corner of the house. He looked closer and saw what very much looked like a Scotsman with a kilt. He had a ferocious appearance and was balancing an axe over one shoulder.

The man shifted slightly as he dozed, wondering if he was imagining what he saw. The Scotsman was pacing, as if he was guarding the house. He kept glaring into the shadows and twirling his axe, waiting for evil-doers to pounce.

The man's view changed, and he suddenly was inside his living room. One of their children must have broken a potato chip bag as they left, leaving crumbs littering the carpet. The television was blaring with late-night cartoons. He and his wife had joked about their choice of the cartoon channel. They had commented that it wouldn't help the atmosphere if shoot 'em up movies were playing while they were gone.

He was surprised in a detached, dreamlike sort of way to see a tall man dressed in a fashionable tee shirt and cotton trousers sitting on the edge of the couch, intently watching the cartoon characters racing across the television screen. The man was quite handsome: clean-shaven and around forty. He leaned forward as he watched the cartoons, with a lively, mobile expression on his face.

After a short time, the stranger rose from the couch, still gazing with great interest at the cartoons, and picked up the hose of a vacuum cleaner. Switching it on, the man pushed the vacuum back and forth across the narrow living room as he continued to stare at the television. The stranger vacuumed the entire room, paying particular attention to the corners.

Gently placing the vacuum down at the edge of the room, the man walked over to the pot-bellied stove where the family's overfed white cat lay watching him with fascination. He bent down, smiling, stroking the cat's chin, making comforting sounds. "Hungry, perhaps?"

The scene blurred for a moment, as the man in the motel room heard a car rudely honk in the parking lot outside the motel room window. As the living room came back into focus, he saw the tall man stoop and noisily pour cat food into a bowl at the edge of the hearth. The cat purred his approval as he walked to the dish.

The living room started to fade, and the man was suddenly outside, once more gazing at the Scotsman standing at attention at the corner of the house. The sky was dark, with a faint swatch of stars struggling against the lights of the nearby shopping center. It was cold, and the street looked lonely, with the streetlights casting a mournful glimmer. Against the illuminated curtains of the house, the man could see the faint shadow of a tall man walking back and forth across the living room.

The man fell asleep then, pressing himself against the warmth of his wife, no longer worried. As the image of their house began to fade, he smiled and murmured a sleepy prayer of thanks to the angel who fed the cat.

Our cat Rupert, the subject of this story.

The Child in the Forest

*T*he thief was a gnarly little creature. When the dust from the old Roman road swirled around him, he seemed to merge into the stones until he resembled nothing more than debris dropped from a passing cart. Only his eyes moved as he watched travelers exit through the gates of the town. He had arrived that morning and had been watching the gates for hours. Since he had not tried to enter the town, the guards had decided to ignore him.

When a small group of travelers rode out in the afternoon, the thief's eyes glinted with pleasure. The merchant riding in the middle was huge, with rolls of fat straining against his velvet tunic, only partially hiding a large purse tied to his belt. His face was stained with sweat and layers of grime, and his eyes were small, engulfed by a face swollen by a life of overeating. The thief watched in fascination as the merchant picked strings of food from broken teeth with fingers that were heavy with rings of gold and rubies. The paradox of jewels embedded in filth was a common sight among the gentry of ninth-century France. Fortunately, from the thief's point of view, precious stones and metals were unharmed by dirt and bits of chicken fat.

The merchant was flanked by women on horseback and foot soldiers carrying bows and swords. The soldiers were glancing at the forest uneasily, clutching the hilts of their swords. Northmen had been attacking travelers more frequently, roaming far from their longboats, killing men and taking women as slaves. Three poorly trained men were little defense against the fury of the Vikings. The women accompanying the merchant seemed unconscious of their danger. Two of them were glaring at him and complaining loudly about the summer heat. From their ages, the thief assumed that one was his wife and the other his daughter. The wife was thin and haughty and unattractive. The daughter might have been pretty, but her petulant demeanor was of the type that drove suitors away in distaste. The women were followed by a maid, who looked equally miserable and sour. The group passed the thief without noticing him and soon was out of sight.

After a short wait, the thief slowly stood up and walked across the road into the woods as if to relieve himself. One of the gatekeepers glanced at him, shrugged, and turned back to his companions. The thief smiled as he disappeared into the trees. His opinion of guards was low, not entirely without reason. Guard duty was frequently a dull and lazy occupation. He found them easy to avoid and easy to fool.

He moved silently through the forest, running swiftly across country in a direction that would bring him out on the road a few miles from the town. He had scouted the road the day before and had decided to move against his quarry as they approached a ford across a river. As he ran, he calculated the value of the rings he had seen. Why was it that so many merchants were fat and stupid? Did they not know that they would be better served if they traveled in rags and took their rings off their hands? In these days, with Northmen crossing the ocean, looking poor was a much safer way to stay alive.

The thief had seen Northmen from a distance once. As he stared from the top of a hill, they had attacked and murdered the inhabitants of a small village. The thief had found it difficult to watch. He abhorred bloodshed and was sickened by the viciousness of the Northmen. He had heard that they sometimes impaled babies on the ends of their spears. A warrior who refused to do so was called a "child lover." The thief's face darkened as he ran. To the thief, any warrior that killed a child was repugnant and inhuman.

His ruminations came to an end as he approached the ford. Positioning himself behind a large tree, he waited patiently, paying no heed to the insects that quickly began feasting on his sweat-covered body. The thief had been toughened in many prisons and had endured far worse discomforts than bugs. His body was covered with so many scars from torture and whippings that his skin resembled leather chewed by dogs. His bones had become crooked, but his strength was still remarkable for one so small. Miraculously, or so his mother might have told him, he had escaped execution. He had not seen the inside of a prison for four years, and he had sworn that he would never be caught again. He had grown cautious and preferred to confront his victims in lonely corners, away from guards and other law-abiding citizens.

A merchant traveling with frightened servants and women was a perfect target for the thief. His methods of theft were not force or murder, but ploys based on cunning and speed. Much to his credit, he had never killed anyone, even when opportunities for more riches had beckoned to him. His infrequent companions had laughed at him for his weakness, but he had stubbornly rejected violence. He never explained his reasons to his fellow brigands, contenting himself with silently honoring the only good memory he had in a life of wandering.

His mother had been an uneducated woman with no family and a standard of morality beset by hardship. Her only assets were a beautiful singing voice and a buxom body that she flaunted with a wicked sense of humor. She had raised him in a small village a few miles from a large town that, to his young eyes, was the most fascinating place on earth. The villagers were endlessly appreciative of her sly wit and her songs but could only offer her gifts of food. Needing money, she began to travel to the town, to sing on the streets and in the taverns. Out of necessity, she took her son with her, not suspecting that the town would be his downfall.

When he was eleven, he handed her a pouch as they walked back through the forest to their home. She had had a difficult time in the town and had spent days struggling against the wiles of a woman who was younger and more beautiful and, most depressingly, a better singer. She took the leather bag from him and weighed it in her hand.

"What is this?" she asked.

He smiled proudly and said, "It is for you, mother."

To his chagrin, the remainder of the walk home was loud and unpleasant. After hearing how he had removed the purse from the waist of a traveler deep in slumber, she cried, and shouted at him, and said a prayer for his soul, and then, much to his surprise, she fastened the pouch beneath the folds of her dress and told him to tell no one.

When he looked at her in wonder, she scolded him angrily, saying, "We cannot return it! I cannot lose you to a prison, or worse."

She made him swear an oath that day that he would never steal again. He cried and nodded in agreement, but the town with its drunken revelers was too easy for his natural talent. He watched his mother grow weary as she made her rounds and soon abandoned his pledge. When he handed her stolen purses on their trips back to the village, she accepted them with resignation and a plea to be careful and not get caught. He nodded and agreed to restrict his activities to departing groups of travelers who would not realize their losses until they had left the town. He learned early on that stealing infrequently, without a discernible pattern, was far safer than the witless greed of less fortunate thieves. His mother's prayers may also have helped, or perhaps it was the blessing of luck, but somehow he managed to avoid detection throughout his youth.

He became proud of his skill over the next year but was shocked one afternoon as they rested on a mossy bank outside their village. He had just turned twelve, and he had begun to think that he was a man. She took his hands in hers and looked at him fiercely, with tears in her eyes, and made him swear that he would never use violence of any kind. He was never to hit anyone or wound or kill a person. He asked her why he couldn't, wondering why stealing a person's money was acceptable to her. Was it not violence of another kind? She scowled, frustrated with her inability to explain.

"I do not like stealing," she said, "especially from those in need. If you must steal, steal only from the rich. They do not miss it that much. But violence is another matter. It is a dreadful sin to kill or maim another. Think of your friend Pepin."

At her words, his façade crumbled, and he stared at the ground, unable to speak. Pepin had been his best friend since they were old enough to bang sticks in the mud. They were the same age, but Pepin had been a handsome youth, with a grin that was so wide it seemed to split his face in two. One day, when they were ten, they had gone into the forest to play. He had tried to keep up with Pepin, but his friend's legs were longer than his, and soon all he could hear was Pepin's voice in the distance, teasing him to run faster.

When he heard Pepin scream, he ran without thinking, crashing through the underbrush, shouting that he was coming. Hearing nothing in reply, he panicked and almost blinded himself on a bramble that swung across his face as he plunged forward. He finally found his friend in a clearing, slumped on the ground next to a path. He sobbed loudly and hysterically when he saw Pepin. The side of his head had been crushed—so viciously that there was no doubt that Pepin was dead.

Except for Pepin's body, the only signs that anyone had been there were some fresh horse droppings on the path. He ran down the trail, furiously trying to catch the man who had killed his friend, but as fast as his short legs could carry him, he was unable to catch up with the murderer. He never discovered Pepin's killer and never found out why the man had so senselessly murdered his friend. The men of the village examined the wound and declared that it was caused by a spiked club, a vicious weapon to use against a defenseless boy. They had shaken their heads sadly, muttering at the evil of such a random deed. His mother had tried to console him, but nothing could take away his feelings of guilt that he had not been there to help his friend when he was attacked.

As he thought about Pepin again, he began to sob until his mother squeezed him against her body and held him close. She kissed his cheek and murmured, "This is why you must never use violence, except to defend yourself or others. Someone will grieve if you do."

He rubbed the tears from his eyes and swore to her that he would obey.

He began to understand her more as he grew older and watched as she sheltered people in need of sustenance. She was a warm and earthy woman, willing to embrace anyone in need. Their hovel was cramped and dark, but she would often bring children home and care for them when they were hungry or had been beaten unjustly. He had watched his mother with respect and love and had been heartbroken when she had died from an illness when he was sixteen.

That seemed like a long time ago, and his life had been crueler and harsher than he had expected. Now in his thirties, he had grown tired and cynical over the years and had strayed quite far from his mother's admonition to steal only from the rich. To him, anyone richer than he was rich enough. His one remaining vestige of pride was that he still had not wounded or murdered any of his victims. He focused his trade on deception and speed. A quick cutting of the purse strings, and he was gone. More often than not, it had worked quite well. He had not yet devised a way to quickly remove finger rings, much to his profound disappointment, especially when the rings were as large as those borne by today's victim.

As the clop, clop of horses sounded in the distance, he prepared himself. Taking a pouch from his belt, he opened it and plunged one hand into the bag. His nose wrinkled in disgust as he pulled out bits of a brown substance and smeared it across his tunic. He had filled the pouch with fresh dog droppings that morning as he approached the town. He had found that his victims were so repulsed by the odor of excrement that they would thus pay less attention to him. Distraction was his favorite weapon.

As the merchant and his retinue rounded a bend in the road and approached the ford, the thief limped out into the road and began to sing. His voice was cracked and off-key, but he sang loudly: a song from the church that he had heard in his travels. The foot soldiers partially unsheathed their swords and glanced at the merchant for guidance. He was bemused and stared at the thief in astonishment.

"What do you here, my man?" he asked. "Why do you stop me?"

He shook his head at the soldiers as the thief drew near. "Put away your swords. He is unarmed. Can you not hear his song and see his balding pate? Perhaps he is a monk, in penance."

His wife and daughter looked askance at the thief and drew their horses aside as he walked between them and placed his hand on the bridle of the merchant's horse. The daughter wrinkled her nose and uttered, "His smell is horrible!"

The merchant coughed and looked down at the thief. "You are offending us with your stench! What is it that you want?"

The thief looked at the merchant and then at the two women. He needed a few moments to decide which items he could steal, which purses he could cut, and still make it to the safety of the woods. He bowed to the merchant and touched his forehead. "I am just a poor mendicant, your Holiness, in penance for my sins. I have been ordered by the friars to sleep with the dogs."

The merchant looked triumphantly at the guards, who were scowling at the thief. "You see! He is in penance!"

The thief crossed himself. "Yes, sire." Straightening, he reached a decision. "My Lord, I see that you are on the road to the court at Aachen. Are you one of the Emperor's great ministers? Perhaps you could offer one silver denier to help me on my journey?"

The merchant's great weakness was that he possessed the inaccurate pride of a buffoon. Immediately responding to the thief's sly compliment, he tried hard to lift his weight and sit straighter in the saddle. Ignoring his wife's snicker, he replied, "Minister? Bah! I am of far greater importance to Charles le Magne. I am not just a simple minister!"

His wife and daughter guffawed in a very unladylike manner. One could tell that they were not at all respectful of the merchant's vanity. He scowled and opened the purse at his belt. Taking a coin from the pouch, he handed it to the thief and said, "Here is your denier, my good man. You may know that I am one of the few men who can finance the Emperor's campaigns!" He glared at his wife and daughter, who both lowered their heads, hiding their smiles.

He turned to address the thief once more and was shocked to see him fleeing toward the forest. He looked at the soldiers in bewilderment, and then at his wife and daughter. His daughter stared at the thief, who was almost at the forest's edge, and then back at her father. Her mouth opened in surprise, and she pointed at his belt. The merchant looked down and saw that his fat purse was no longer at his waist. The thief had sliced it from his belt and had run in the single moment that the merchant had glared at his wife and daughter.

His face was violently purple as he shouted at his men. They were fumbling with their swords and their bows when the daughter cried out in terror. She was pointing toward the ford, her face stricken with fear. Just entering the shallow water were two Northmen, walking casually, with their axes slung over their shoulders. When they saw the merchant and his party, they let out a harsh battle cry and started pushing their way through the water toward the road.

The thief had already entered the forest when he heard their cries. He crept back to the edge of the woods and carefully looked out from under a bush. One of the foot soldiers had grabbed the reins of the daughter's horse and had reached the edge of the woods on the other side of the road. As he and the daughter fled into the forest, the thief looked back toward the rest of the group. A soldier was trying to guide the wife into the woods as well, but the wife pushed him away and went to her husband, who was circling his horse in terror and confusion. The remaining foot soldier had managed to pull a shaft from his quiver, and as the Northmen came up to them, he let the arrow fly. One of the Northmen fell, with the arrow in his stomach, and, at first, it seemed that the merchant's men might win the day. However, it was not to be, for the second Northman was in a fury and swung his axe with such ruthlessness that soon the road was strewn with the bodies of the merchant and his men. Only the maid and the wife were left alive, gazing in horror at the Northman as he approached them. He was a large man with a dreadfully scarred face and one eye. A gray and wrinkled hollow lay where his other eye should have been.

The thief inched his way back into the forest as the Northman hauled the two women off their horses and proceeded to beat them and kick them, cursing at them loudly. He was covered in blood and was shouting in rage. The thief shook his head sadly as he crept deeper into the woods and finally broke into a run. The fate of the women would not be pleasant, although it was likely that they would live.

The thief lived in dread of the Northmen. The raiders were so savage and brutal that being seen by them was very close to a death sentence. Few escaped their rapid and merciless assaults. It was thus that the thief ran that day without a plan and without reason. He didn't think that he had been sighted, but where there was one Northman, there were usually more. Their boats had a shallow three-foot draft that allowed the invaders to push deep into the mainland, traveling up rivers where none expected them to come.

The thief had run east into the forest, and, after an hour, he realized that he was quite lost. The woods were thick, with trees that were huge and menacing. The sun was getting lower in the sky, and the thief began to panic. He had heard of men getting lost in the dark forests and never returning. His thoughts grew turbulent, and he began to breathe heavily. Climbing up a small hill, he cursed as he got tangled in a wall of vines. He began beating against the vines and tried to cut them with his dirk, crying out in frustration and anger.

He was chopping furiously at a vine when the earth crumbled beneath him, and he started to slide down the other side of the hill. He tried to catch himself, but the ground was covered with moss and dead leaves, and he couldn't find a footing. He slipped and fell and swore as he bruised himself against rocks until, finally, his descent was halted with a splash next to a large, jagged rock. He had landed in a stream and was now sitting in rapidly moving water, looking at the rock that might have split his brains in half.

He sat there, dazed, in shock from the Northmen's attack, ignoring the water splashing over his knees. When he heard the voice, he thought that perhaps it was a wood sprite. He had heard about them and their mischievous ways.

"You are a strange little man."

He looked up, afraid. "Who spoke?" he cried.

The imp laughed. "I did, little man." The creature's speech was small and tinkly, like that of a child. Perhaps wood sprites sounded like children. Evil children, to be sure.

"Show yourself!" he demanded. He struggled to his feet and slipped and fell down again with a splash.

The creature laughed again, loudly this time. Suddenly, small hands covered his eyes. The hands were attached to arms that encircled his head. He was sure that at the very next moment, he would be tied up and carried off by this evil sprite. He wrenched himself free from the hands and stumbled forward, and then turned around to face his attacker.

There, standing in the stream, was a child. He was dressed in a tunic and leggings and seemed like an ordinary boy except that his tunic was embroidered with silken thread, and he carried a small sword with a jeweled hilt at his belt. He had long, fair hair and lively eyes. He was laughing at the thief's expression of surprise.

"You are very wet," he said.

The thief nodded in agreement and started to shiver as the boy turned toward the far bank of the stream and said, "Come with me. We have a fire for you to warm yourself."

The thief hesitated. The boy didn't look like a Northman, but one couldn't be sure who were friends in times like these. The boy turned and beckoned him forward. "Come," he said. "We will not hurt you."

The boy paused and wrinkled his nose. "Could you rinse off your tunic? You have the most awful smell of the droppings of dogs."

The thief had to agree. He rarely bathed, but the smell of dog excrement was indeed vile. As he splashed water across the front of his tunic, he glanced at the boy. Was he an evil sprite, luring him to his death?

It was the chill of his clothes and the hunger in his belly that persuaded the thief to trust the boy. He scrambled after him, up the bank to a small clearing that was surrounded by huge and ancient trees. The sun barely made its way through the heavy branches, and, at first, he found it difficult to see through the gloom. As his vision adjusted, he started in surprise and considered turning to run. Sitting against the base of a tree was a knight. He was holding a knife in his hand and was staring fiercely at the thief. A tall horse was quietly nibbling on the sparse grass at the foot of the tree.

The boy ran to him and exclaimed, "No, no, you cannot sit up. Do not worry. The little man will not hurt us." He took the knight's shoulders and helped him lie down. The knight's eyes stayed fastened on the thief, even while the knife dropped to the ground. The thief could see that he was severely wounded, with a deep gash in his side. His chain mail and shield and weapons lay next to him. The knight whispered something, and the child leaned closer to hear. Turning to the thief, the boy said, "He wants to know who you are."

The thief looked at the fire burning in the middle of the clearing and asked, "May I warm myself at your fire?"

The boy nodded, and the thief removed his long tunic and placed it on sticks next to the fire. He had several pouches tied to a rope around the waist of his trousers, and after a long look at the knight and the boy, he untied the rope and placed the pouches on the ground next to his tunic. He was shivering and rubbed his hands over the fire in relief.

He didn't answer the boy for a few moments, until the boy grew impatient and demanded, "You must answer the knight's question!"

It was a dilemma for the thief. He had hidden from everyone in authority for years and had always kept his name a secret. Not knowing who the knight was, he decided not to reveal himself, even though it seemed that he was in no real danger from the knight or the boy.

Looking up from the fire, he said, "I cannot say. My name is only for those I trust. And I trust no one."

The boy looked exasperated and bent down again to listen to the knight. Looking at the thief, he said, "The knight asks you to come closer, so he can see your face."

The thief shrugged and walked over to the knight. Squatting on his haunches, he stared at the knight. "Well?" he asked.

The knight was a young man, with a straight nose and a strong jaw. His eyes were blue and very steady as he stared at the thief. He stared for a long moment until the thief began to fidget. Suddenly the knight relaxed and looked at the child and nodded. The boy said, "You can stand up now."

The thief went back to the fire and warmed himself again, staring at the knight, trying to understand what had happened. The boy came over to the fire and handed the thief a piece of meat and a cup of ale. "Eat," he said. The thief obliged him, with a grateful smile.

The boy suddenly took out his sword and held it to the thief's naked chest, almost causing the thief to drop the cup of ale. "Will you betray us?" the boy asked.

The Child in the Forest

The thief thought for a moment, then shook his head. "No."

"Swear to me that you will not," the boy demanded. "Swear on what is precious to you."

The thief paused again and then replied, "I swear on the memory of my mother. But is there a reason to betray you?"

At that, the boy drew himself up as tall as he could and declared, "Only to the Northmen. But you are not a Northman, are you?"

"No," said the thief. He shuddered. "Certainly not."

The boy sheathed his sword, satisfied. He pointed at the knight, who had been watching the exchange. "This is Bero. He is my faithful servant and a noble knight in my grandfather's court."

"Your grandfather?" asked the thief.

The boy smiled and thrust his chest out in pride. "My grandfather is King Charles, the Emperor of the Romans," he said. "My name is Nithard. My father is Angilbert, the Abbot of the monastery of Centula, and my mother is Bertha, the daughter of the Emperor." He looked at the thief and said even more grandly, "I was born in December of the year of our Lord, 795, just five years before my grandfather became Emperor."

The thief chewed on a bit of meat while he thought about this information. "So, you are ten," he said. "I was ten once." Draining his cup, he burped and waved his hand toward the knight. "What happened to him?" he asked.

Nithard gazed sadly at the knight. "Bero and his men were bringing me back from Centula to my mother's home in Aachen. We were attacked by Northmen, and they killed his men and almost killed Bero and me. But we escaped into the forest on Bero's steed. Bero knows this forest well, from hunting trips."

Bero had been watching Nithard with a faint smile on his lips as the boy had strutted in front of the thief. It was clear, however, that his strength was failing him. He started to cough and gasped for air. Nithard went to him and took his hand. Looking at the thief, he cried, "Is there nothing you can do?"

The thief shook his head. There was nothing anyone could do. He had seen death too many times and knew that the knight would never leave the forest. As it was, he felt pity for the boy, so he went to the knight's side and looked at the wound. The boy had tried to dress it, but it was a deep gash, and Bero had lost a great deal of blood. It was a wonder that the knight was still alive. He was examining the injury when the knight clutched his arm and whispered hoarsely. The thief bent forward, straining to hear.

"You must help the boy," Bero whispered.

The thief gazed at the knight, perplexed. Bero stared at him with a pleading look. "I have sworn a sacred oath to keep Nithard safe, but I will die here. He cannot make it to Aachen by himself. The Northmen are roaming everywhere."

The thief shook his head vehemently. "I cannot go to Aachen," he said.

The knight squeezed his wrist fiercely. "You must go! The boy is precious to the Emperor. You cannot let him die."

"I cannot go to Aachen," said the thief. He shook his head and pulled his arm from Bero's grasp.

Nithard had been watching their interchange and looked at the thief in wonder. "Why is it that you cannot go to Aachen?" he asked. "Everyone wants to visit the court at Aachen. The whole world wants to see the great Emperor Charlemagne."

The thief stood up and nervously stepped to the fire. He was shivering again and put more wood on the fire until it was roaring loudly. The light from the flames bounced crazily against the canopy of trees. Night had fallen, and the forest seemed very grim to the thief. Bero and Nithard watched him as he pulled on his shirt. He was a sad figure of a man: only four feet in height, alarmingly bony, and rather hideous. Stringy, gray hair did little to hide a head that was angular and sharp, punctuated by a broken nose and swollen lips that framed a mouth warped in a grimace. His chest was covered with scars, but his torso was surprisingly muscular, with arms that were wiry and strong.

When he realized that the knight and the boy were watching him, he paused as he tied the pouches around his waist. He stared back at them for a moment and then continued to adjust the rope. His eyes were large and brown and flickered with sadness under a hardened veneer. He was fumbling self-consciously and cursed as he struggled with an uncooperative knot that suddenly slipped from his grasp. He tried to catch the rope but was unable to stop the bags from falling to the ground. When the largest pouch hit the ground, its tie loosened, and silver coins spilled from its mouth onto the earth.

The knight was too weak to move, but Nithard stared in fascination at the silver. The thief looked at Nithard and Bero and then looked at the deniers at his feet. With a sigh, he bent down and picked up the coins and the fine leather pouch, and said, "This is why I cannot go to Aachen."

Nithard looked puzzled and then bent down to hear the knight's whisper. He straightened and put one hand on his sword. "You are a thief?" he asked.

"Yes," said the thief. "I cannot go to Aachen because I escaped from its dungeons. If I go back, they will torture and kill me. I cannot go back."

Bero motioned to the boy, who bent close to his chest and listened attentively. He nodded and then looked at the thief. "Bero believes that you came to us under the grace of God. He knows how vast this forest is and knows that chance would not have brought you to us. Chance would have led you past us, and we would have no help at all. I was in the stream for only a few moments to get water for Bero. But you came just at that moment. Bero believes the Virgin brought you to us. He said that therefore you must take me to Aachen."

Nithard stared down at Bero and suddenly stomped the ground angrily. "And he must take you, also, Bero! I will not leave you here!"

Bero smiled weakly and whispered something as he squeezed the boy's knee. The thief couldn't hear what he said, but it didn't satisfy Nithard, who looked up at the thief and cried, "You must help us!"

The thief shrugged sadly and said, "I cannot go to Aachen."

Nithard banged his fist against the ground and said, "You have told us that!" He glared at the thief angrily and ground out his words, "What shall I call you then? Thief? Shall I just call you 'thief?' Is that all you are?"

The thief's face flushed, and he looked away. "You may call me thief if you like."

"Then thief it is!" spat Nithard. "Thief, can you bring Bero water? He is growing faint."

The thief silently picked up a cup and dipped it into a large bowl of water on the ground. He carried it to Nithard and handed it to him without a word. Returning to the fire, he sat down with his back against a stump and closed his eyes. He felt drained, weary in both body and soul.

Nithard gently gave the water to Bero, who struggled to drink. Most of the water ran from the corners of his mouth. He was pale and in a great deal of pain. He slowly lifted his hand and touched Nithard's cheek, and gazed at him affectionately. It was too much for the boy. He sobbed and started to throw himself across Bero's chest but then realized that it would hurt the knight's wound. In frustration, he took Bero's hands and kissed them. The thief opened one eye when he heard the boy crying and watched him for a moment. With a painful twist of his mouth, he turned his head away and tried once more to sleep.

The fire slowly died down, and the boy fell asleep next to Bero, holding his hand. The thief was less fortunate and woke frequently, listening to Bero's labored breathing and inadvertent moans of pain. As the first glimmer of morning sun struggled through the dense treetops, Bero cried out, saying something in Latin, which the thief couldn't understand. His breath came in huge, rattling gasps, and while Nithard and the thief watched, the knight looked straight up at the trees and died.

Nithard was exhausted, unable to cry. Instead, he rocked back and forth, saying, "No, no, no, no," choking and gasping between his murmurs. The thief took him a cup of water, but Nithard ignored him. The thief set the cup next to the boy and went back to the fire, and built it up again. He checked the saddlebags next to the horse and discovered a small amount of smoked beef and one remaining leather flask of ale. It was very little food for an arduous journey through the forest to Aachen.

The thief went down to the stream and proceeded to haul dozens of boulders and small rocks up to the clearing. Finally, satisfied, he went to Nithard and placed his hand on the boy's shoulder. Nithard looked up with an expression of grief that the thief remembered well.

"We have to bury him now," said the thief. He angrily brushed his hand across his eyes. He didn't want to think about Pepin or his feelings as he and his mother had prayed over his grave.

Nithard stood up without a word. They straightened Bero's body at the foot of the tree. Nithard removed a ring from Bero's hand and the pouches from his belt and then took Bero's sword and scabbard and other weapons and placed them next to the horse with Bero's belongings. Finally, he went to the edge of the stream and picked some wildflowers and laid them over Bero's wound. Still not speaking, he began piling the stones on top of Bero's body. They worked together until Bero's entire body was covered except his face. It was then that Nithard broke down again.

Crouching down, he looked at Bero and then sidelong at the thief, trying manfully to hide the tears rolling down his cheeks. "He was assigned to me when I was born," he said. "He was my best and truest friend."

The thief stood quietly until Nithard rose and went to the remaining rocks and picked up a large stone. He moved to help Nithard, but the boy waved him away. Nithard gently placed the stone over Bero's face and then laid the rest of the rocks around it. When he was done, he knelt and prayed and made the sign of the cross, and finally kissed the very top stone.

Rising, he looked at the thief, who had remained standing all the while, and asked, "Where do you go now?"

"Aachen," said the thief.

The boy looked surprised but simply nodded. They put out the fire and watered the horse at the stream. The thief handed the small piece of beef to the boy, who refused it. Placing it back in the saddlebag, he looked at Nithard and said, "I know that Aachen is to the north, but I am not certain which path to take to find our way out of this forest."

Nithard pointed upstream. "We fled east when the Northmen attacked us. Bero told me that if we follow this stream toward the north for a day, we'll come to a waterfall and a valley that goes west. If we follow that, we'll connect again to the road to Aachen that comes from Centula. He said that it would take us less than two days by horseback to reach my grandfather's court."

"Let us follow the stream, then," said the thief.

He helped Nithard tie Bero's weapons to the saddle. Since he would be riding behind Nithard, it was difficult to carry everything, but they didn't want to leave the weapons behind. Nithard slung his small bow and quiver of arrows around his chest and hung their throwing axes from each side of the saddle. They had four axes—Bero and Nithard had each carried two. The thief picked one up and was surprised by its weight. It was a Frankish axe, with a wooden shaft that was a foot and a half long and a heavy iron head that measured six inches across with a four-inch curved blade that ended in wicked-looking points. They were extremely sharp.

Bero's sword was awkward, with its three and a half foot length, but they finally wrapped it in a cloth and tied it behind the saddle.

Nithard was an accomplished rider and mounted the horse quickly, even though he had to stand on a rock to reach the stirrups. Once in the saddle, he extended his arm to help the thief, who was scowling and having a difficult time of it. The thief was not a rider and didn't like horses, preferring animals that were cooked. Riding behind Nithard without the benefit of the saddle was even more nerve-racking. As Nithard guided the horse along the edge of the stream, he clutched the boy's tunic until Nithard protested that he was holding it too tightly.

They traveled slowly, for there was no path except the stream, and they had to dismount frequently and walk the steed through dense undergrowth. Fortunately, the water was not deep, so for the most part, they kept to the center of the stream. They traveled for many hours, drinking sparingly, and finally sharing the last morsel of dried beef in the late afternoon. They were famished and decided that they must stop to find food before nightfall.

As they rode, Nithard talked of Bero's skill as a hunter and, for a brief moment, seemed to forget that his friend was dead. Nithard laughed boastfully when he said that Bero had taught him to throw his axes with such skill that Nithard had once been able to kill a small boar. He lifted his arms and clenched his biceps to show the thief his strength. The thief nodded in some surprise.

"You look exceedingly strong for one so young. But is it not easier to hunt with your bow?"

"That is true," Nithard replied. "But a throwing axe is a very good weapon. Have you used one? Or a sword or bow?"

The thief shook his head. "No, none of them."

"Then, I shall teach you how to throw an axe," said Nithard. "And I will use the bow to hunt. Bero told me that this forest is plentiful with animals."

They decided to stop by a wide area of the stream, in a clearing under a willow tree. They tied the horse to a stump, where it munched contentedly on the grass growing from the bank of the stream. Nithard showed the thief how to hold the axe by the shaft and bring it back over his head and then forward with great force. He set the thief to practicing in front of a tree, with the four axes, and then left him, walking upstream to hunt for food.

The sun was fading behind the trees when Nithard returned, carrying a rabbit and a small wild pig. He was grinning broadly and immediately started to build a fire. He looked at the thief and asked, "Well? Did you sink the blades in the tree?"

The thief had worked very hard in Nithard's absence and responded by throwing all four axes into the massive oak. He wasn't very far from the tree, and the shafts turned over only once, but it was still an accomplishment. Nithard applauded him, and soon they were eating hungrily by the fire. They made short work of the rabbit and ate a tremendous amount of the pig before they talked again.

Finally, wiping his mouth on his sleeve, Nithard looked at the thief with a solemn gaze and said, "I have trusted you, and now you are helping me. Is it not time that you told me your name?"

The thief sat for a long moment, looking into the fire. He had not told anyone his real name for many years, even under torture. When one is tortured by someone who doesn't know your name, any name will do to stop the pain. He had adopted a different name when his mother had died, out of respect for her memory. His real name was precious to her, and thus to him. He had wanted to preserve it as a part of himself that belonged to her and to a better life, long ago. Since then, he had either used a false name or no name at all, preferring anonymity.

Now, staring into the beauty of the flames, he realized that no one had asked him for help for a very long time. He had been shunned and kicked and spat upon. He had been chased and tortured and had lived alone, unwanted and unnoticed by the world. To have a knight and the grandson of an emperor trust him and look to him for help was beyond his imagination. It felt strange to him, but very pleasing.

Turning to the boy, he said, "My mother was Chlotilde, a village woman. She named me Theodoric. She said it was my father's name and told me about him many times. He was a wandering storyteller and could make a whole village laugh or cry. He and my mother were fascinated with each other and finally married. I think she was very wild. She often coaxed him to the river where they would secretly swim in the moonlight. He didn't want to take off his clothes, but she teased him to disrobe. He was ashamed because his height was that of a child, and he was thin and weak, and from all accounts extremely ugly."

He flushed and stared at the fire. "Like me, actually, except that I am unexpectedly strong."

After a moment, he continued. "My mother said that on the night that I was conceived, a terrible thing happened. They swam in the river and were very happy, lying on the riverbank, watching the clouds move across the sky. Then, on the way back to the village, running across the fields, he tripped and fell, cutting his leg very badly on a piece of metal. She carried him back to her hut and tried to nurse him, but after a few days, his leg became swollen and dark in color. Soon his whole body was hot to the touch, and he stiffened in pain and shouted mad things. And then he died. She grieved for many months. She gave me his name because she loved him. But I have not used that name since she died, when

I was sixteen. She was not happy that I was a thief, and I did not want to dishonor her."

Nithard was silent for a long moment. Taking a sip of water, he said, "I am sorry about your father."

The thief looked at him gratefully. "Thank you."

Nithard brightened and said, "My father told me many tales of the past. There was a great king named Theodoric, but I cannot remember more than that."

They sat for a while in silence. The thief felt exceedingly strange. To reveal his name after so many years was emotionally confusing. To hear that it was a king's name made him feel faintly dizzy. Although he considered the idea that his dizziness was from eating a surfeit of roast pig. His reverie was interrupted by Nithard.

"Shall I call you Theodoric?"

The thief nodded. "If you wish," he replied. "But please do not tell my name to others."

Nithard agreed and watched thankfully as the thief placed more logs on the fire.

Theodoric looked at Nithard inquiringly. "Do we need to keep watch?" he asked.

Nithard shook his head. "Bero said that the Northmen do not venture this deep into the forest. They travel quickly along the roads, seeking easy plunder. They will not see our fire here."

Theodoric sat down next to him and replied, "For that, I am glad indeed." He yawned, and grinned at Nithard. "Too much pig," he said.

Soon both the boy and the thief were sound asleep, stretched out in front of the fire.

⋘ ⋘ ⋘

They woke with the dawn. Theodoric rose first and prepared the horse, while Nithard put out the fire. After eating quickly, they mounted their steed and turned upriver once again.

They had traveled only a few miles when they came to a high waterfall. They were at first disheartened, wondering how they would guide the horse around it, but then they saw that Bero's directions had been correct. To their left lay a broad valley, sloping down out of the forest to a road. Nithard looked at Theodoric with an excited smile.

"It is the road to Aachen!" he exclaimed.

Theodoric stared at the distant road with a feeling of dismay. Now that he was so close to Aachen, he began to have doubts about his course of action. As they guided the horse down a steep path toward the valley, he considered turning back. The boy was walking in front of him, holding the reins in one hand, while in the other he held a walking stick that he had cut. The way was difficult, with loose rocks and pebbles making the footing treacherous.

As Theodoric gazed at the boy, his feelings grew confused. For many years he had looked at the wealthy and powerful as targets and had treated them with a remoteness of heart that allowed him to steal from them without guilt. He had never stolen from a child, but many times children had been present when he stole from their parents. He had looked at them without seeing them, unable to open his senses to their reality. To be walking behind a boy he was trying to help was something he had never expected.

He had been impressed with the boy's bravery, both before and after Bero's death. Nithard's spirit was valiant and reminded the thief of his own experience after his mother died. He was surprised that he genuinely liked the boy. As if he felt Theodoric's thoughts, Nithard looked back at him and smiled. Theodoric wasn't used to smiling but did his best to muster a grin.

Nithard pointed his walking stick in front of him and said, "Look! We have a clear path from here. We can ride."

They had come to an outcrop of rock. Below them was a broad path that must have been used by many hunting parties. It stretched down to the floor of the valley, and then on through fields and woods to the Roman road beyond. They stood for a few moments, searching the land for any signs of Northmen. All seemed peaceful, so they mounted the horse and slowly picked their way down the path. Theodoric's nervousness increased, and he clutched Nithard's tunic until his hand ached.

He looked at the throwing axes bumping against the horse's side and wondered if he would have to use them. He had never felt particularly brave, even though he had managed to withstand torture. Usually, when he saw knights or foot soldiers, he would creep away as quietly as possible. His small size and ugliness of countenance had been a great help to him since very few ever considered him to be a threat.

When they reached the bottom of the valley, and the path became flat, Nithard urged the horse into a trot. Nithard spoke over his shoulder, saying, "The road is not far now, and Aachen is a short distance beyond. We are almost home!"

Theodoric didn't respond and clutched Nithard's tunic even tighter. He was very close to jumping off the horse and fleeing into the forest. With Aachen so near, he saw little reason why he should continue with the boy and condemn himself to prison and death.

They rode without speaking, trotting down a broad track under magnificent old oak trees. It was a glorious morning, with a light breeze moving across the fields on either side of the path. They splashed through a stream and then saw the road in front of them. Nithard slowed the horse to a walk, and they quietly moved up to the edge of the road. They looked at each other nervously and then stared to their left and right, searching for signs of danger.

To their great relief, the road was empty. They saw no signs that anyone had passed recently—no hoofprints and no horse droppings. To the south, and their left, the road led back to the area where Bero and Nithard had been attacked. A few miles farther down the road was the ford where the merchant and his men had met their death, and beyond that was the small town where the merchant had eaten his last meal. Nithard shuddered as he gazed down the road to the south. He shook his head sadly and swung the horse to the right, north toward Aachen.

Theodoric felt dazed as they rode north. It seemed to him that he had been with Nithard for a long time. It was hard to grasp that he had met the boy only two days before. His inner turmoil increased as they rode, and his general feeling of uneasiness grew intense. As they rode, the forest gradually gave way to fields with thatched cottages. They were surprised that they saw no one about. The windows of the small hovels were shuttered, and even the animals were absent.

Nithard looked at Theodoric with a worried expression. "I have come this way many times with Bero and with my father. I have never seen it like this."

They continued riding, growing more worried with every mile. As they rode to the top of a small hill, a short distance from Aachen, they stopped in shock and quickly moved the horse to the right side of the road, behind a tree. Ahead of them, cottages on both sides of the road were in flames. Northmen were running among the huts, swinging their axes and swords at the peasants with horrifying results. Nithard and Theodoric slowly moved the horse farther into the trees, watching the road all the while. To their great relief, they had not been seen.

Nithard's face was pale as he watched the slaughter in front of them. Theodoric looked at him and suddenly realized that all of this was new to Nithard. He had forgotten that Nithard was only ten and probably had never seen battle before. He touched the boy's shoulder sympathetically and said, "We should go into the forest. We must go around them."

Nithard nodded silently and was turning the horse toward the woods when he stopped and pointed. Far up the road to the north, they could see the glint of chain mail and the movement of horses. Nithard stared for a long moment and then looked at Theodoric with excitement. "It must be a company of knights from my grandfather's court!"

Theodoric strained to make out the details in the cloud of dust coming down the road toward the Northmen. His eyes were not as good as the boy's, but he could see what looked like a large company of knights. He couldn't see how many there were, but it seemed that there were many more knights than there were Northmen. He nodded at Nithard and said, "Let us leave them to the fight. We cannot help from where we are."

Nithard hesitated. "We must join them," he said. "And fight. It is what a warrior would do."

Theodoric shook his head vehemently. "No! We cannot. We will be killed if we fight them from this side. We must go around the Northmen, through the woods, and come out behind the knights. If you want to fight with them after that, you can."

He looked at the boy for a long moment, and then at the beckoning forest. He felt trapped and wanted very badly to run into the trees and disappear. He turned back to the boy, sitting in front of him on the horse. Nithard was tense, biting his lip and spasmodically clutching at his sword hilt. He seemed frightened but also angry and ready for a fight.

After a moment, Nithard nodded and reluctantly turned the horse toward the forest. They rode slowly, carefully, anxious to avoid the noise of branches breaking under the hooves of their horse. They went straight into the woods and then turned north. As they rode, Theodoric's soul grew heavier and more tortured. He had lived entirely for himself since his mother died. After her death, he had never seen any reason to sacrifice for anyone. His life had resembled an abandoned tomb, without illumination or a higher purpose of any kind. Now, as they got closer and closer to the group of knights who undoubtedly would welcome Nithard with open arms, he felt angry that his life might be over. He would be condemned, tortured, and put to death as a thief, and that was all.

Yet, when he looked at the boy sitting in front of him, he couldn't stomach the idea of abandoning him. He vividly imagined the Northmen making short work of the boy, cutting off his head with one blow of an axe, as he had seen them do before. He had heard that they had created a sword stroke called the butterfly cut, in which they sliced open a victim's back in such a way that his lungs fell out, fluttering to the ground like a butterfly. He shuddered as he stared at Nithard's back and imagined that happening to the child. It was a horrifying thought.

It was his memory of Nithard's tears at the death of Bero that created Theodoric's resolve. He could not let the boy die, as Pepin had perished, even if it cost him his life. He gazed at the trees overhead, with the sunshine sparkling down through the leaves, and wondered if he were crazed. He knew that he was not, so he simply sighed and turned his attention to the path in front of them.

He tapped Nithard on the shoulder and whispered, "Do you think that we have gone far enough?"

The boy nodded and reined the horse in. They sat for a moment, staring through the trees to their left. They couldn't see the road but knew that it was less than half a mile away. Nithard looked at Theodoric nervously and asked, "How shall we proceed?"

Theodoric smiled reassuringly and patted the boy's arm. "Follow me, Nithard. I am very good at creeping through woods without being seen. But we must leave the horse behind. It is too big, and we may have to crawl through the bushes on our bellies."

They dismounted and tied the horse to a tree. They didn't want to leave the animal trapped like that but could not risk him following them. Nithard kissed the horse and whispered, "We will try to come back for you."

Theodoric doubted that they would ever see the poor animal again but busied himself with adjusting the axes in his belt, two on each side of his waist. After a few moments, they were ready. As they stood there, it seemed to Theodoric that their weapons were futile. If the Northmen saw them before they could reach the Emperor's knights, they stood little chance of surviving. He tried one last time to dissuade the boy. He pointed north and said, "We do not have to do this. We can travel north and come out on the road far behind the knights, and travel on to your grandfather's court. I am sure that he would prefer that you not die needlessly."

Nithard flushed with a mixture of embarrassment and anger. "My grandfather values courage and would be ashamed of me if I did not assist his knights in battle!" Theodoric opened his mouth to speak, but the boy raised a hand. "No! Bero died saving me. I will not run away. If you do not wish to come, then you may leave by any route you choose."

Theodoric didn't respond or look at the boy. He slowly drank from a leather flask they had refilled in the stream and wiped his mouth on his sleeve. Handing the flask to Nithard, he said, "Drink then, and follow me."

The boy drank silently and handed the pouch back to Theodoric. Without speaking, they turned toward the road and began walking carefully from tree to tree. After a short distance, the trees started to thin, and they could see fields ahead and smell the smoke of burning cottages. The sounds of fighting were faint at first, but as they crept closer, the sounds grew louder, until they could hear screams, and the thud of axes, and the sharp crack of swords against metal and bone.

Falling to their bellies, they moved closer very slowly, until they were at the edge of a clearing. The road was just two hundred yards away, but in between their hiding place and the road was a melee of knights and Northmen hurling themselves at each other in furious combat. The Northmen's axes were brutally effective, and it seemed to Nithard and Theodoric that the knights were close to defeat. Many knights had died, and many knights were terribly wounded, falling to the ground with legs and arms severed by the fierceness of their enemy's blows.

It was difficult to see the field, for the smoke from the cottages was thick. Theodoric bent his head close to Nithard's ear and whispered, "Look! The Northmen are also weakened! There are very few left alive."

In fact, there were less than a dozen still standing, but they were among the most ferocious warriors that Theodoric had ever seen. They seemed possessed by the devil as they swirled in circles around the embattled knights. Theodoric's mouth twitched in fear as he watched the Northmen. He recognized one of the warriors. It was the same man who had killed the merchant. His scarred face and vacant eye socket were covered in blood, but Theodoric was sure it was the same man. He was screaming at the knights as he struck at them and cursing them in his native tongue.

The knights were greater in number than the Northmen, but they were losing, dispirited in heart, and in danger of being completely routed. They seemed to be leaderless and confused. As Theodoric watched them, he was startled by Nithard's abrupt movement next to him. The boy stood up, with his sword over his head, and screamed, "For the Emperor! For my grandfather!" Before Theodoric could stop him, he started to run toward the battle, yelling over and over, "For the Emperor! For my grandfather!"

The Northmen paused for the briefest of moments and saw that it was only a boy running toward them, a boy with a toy sword. One of them pointed at Nithard and barked an order. The man with one eye yelled assent and started walking toward Nithard, swinging his axe. Theodoric looked at the Northman in horror and then, without realizing what he was doing, sprang forward, running to overtake Nithard before the Northman could reach him.

Theodoric had spent a lifetime running away from danger, and in so doing, he had developed exceptionally strong leg muscles. His legs were short, but they carried him amazingly quickly. Now, with the image of the Northman filling his vision, he ran faster than he had ever run before. Soon he had passed Nithard, screaming over his shoulder at the boy, "Go back! Go back!" He didn't wait to see if he had been obeyed but instead ran directly at the Northman.

As he ran, he lifted his axes from his belt, one after the other, and threw them at the Northman with all his strength.

The Northman laughed at the strange little man running toward him and laughed again as the first two axes flew past his head. He cursed and stumbled slightly as the third axe thudded against his shield. Distracted, he failed to counter the final axe, which lodged in his thigh. Then, Theodoric was striking at him with his dirk, awkwardly stabbing at the Northman's body.

The knights had not ignored Nithard's battle cries. As he emerged from the forest, one of them recognized him and shouted to the others, "It is Nithard, the grandson of the Emperor!"

They watched the boy as he ran toward the Northmen, his sword held high, and his long, blond hair streaming behind him. It is at such moments that warriors can sometimes transcend the agony of their wounds and the fear in their hearts and become magnificent spiritual beings. It is at such moments that the size and strength of the enemy become irrelevant. The knights could not explain what happened to them when they saw the boy. All they knew was that they would not let Nithard die that day. Instinctively, they divided into two groups, with one group holding the line against the Northmen, and the second group running toward the single Northman with his axe.

As they ran, they saw Theodoric charge the Northman. They shouted at Nithard to go back, but the boy ignored them and ran to join Theodoric in his attack, lifting his sword to strike. The Northman had regained his footing and swung his axe viciously at Nithard. His axe knocked Nithard's sword from his grasp, spinning the weapon to the ground. Nithard was reaching for a knife as the Northman swung his axe again, this time at Nithard's head.

If the axe had reached Nithard, it would have separated the boy's head from his body. It crashed instead against Theodoric's upraised left arm, severing it just below the elbow. Theodoric was between the Northman and Nithard but had not had time to do more than push Nithard out of the way and raise his arm to shield the boy. Theodoric screamed in agony at the blow and sank to the ground, with blood streaming from the stump of his forearm. He looked up at the Northman, who was preparing to strike again, and resigned himself to finally meeting death.

As Theodoric's vision blurred, he saw the head of the Northman fly from his shoulders, followed by the gleam of a knight's sword. As the thief collapsed into what he thought was death, his mouth twisted upward in a small but satisfied smile.

Theodoric did not wake as the knights killed the remaining Northmen on the field. He was unaware of the care they took as they stopped his arm from bleeding and gently lifted him onto a makeshift litter. Nithard rode next to him as the knights bore their wounded and their dead back to the Emperor's court. It wasn't until Charlemagne stood over Theodoric's body that he finally regained consciousness.

"Is this the man?"

Theodoric struggled to open his eyes. He couldn't move his body, which frightened him greatly.

The voice asked again, "Is this the man?"

With a tremendous effort, he opened his eyes and looked up at a crowd of people gazing down at him. A giant of a man towered over him. The man asked again, "I said, is this the man!"

"Yes, Sire," someone answered. "This is the man who saved Nithard."

Theodoric looked up at the man they called Sire. He had never seen King Charles, even though he had spent an unfortunate amount of time in one of his dungeons. To be stared at by the Emperor of the Romans was intimidating indeed. He tried to get up and realized again that he couldn't move. He was able to turn his head, and thus he could see that he was surrounded by a crowd of knights and women of the court, all looking at him with a high degree of interest. He was flat on his back and bound to a litter that had been placed on the stone floor of what must have been an anteroom of the Emperor's court. He pushed against his restraints once more and felt a stabbing pain in his left elbow. With the pain, his memory of the battle came rushing back, and he strained to see where his forearm should have been.

A woman bent over him and placed her hand on his forehead. She smiled at him and said, "Do not move. We have tied you to your pallet because your movement was making your arm bleed. Our good knights bound your wound tightly, to stop the bleeding, and brought you and Nithard here to court. It is a miracle that you live."

She smiled again warmly and said, "Yes, Nithard is here. Look! My son is standing to your right."

Theodoric turned his head and saw Nithard grinning down at him. The boy crouched down next to him and said, "We have won! The knights killed all of the Northmen after you saved me, and now we are finally home. And they got Bero's horse, too!"

Theodoric smiled wanly at Nithard and looked at the woman again. "Will I not die from my wound, from rot or fever?" he asked. "I have seen it before."

The Emperor answered him in a loud and commanding voice. "You will not!" He looked at the woman and said, "Bertha, you must heal this man." He turned and stared at the crowd of knights and ladies and pointed down at Theodoric. "Mark this man well! This broken little man challenged a Northman almost twice his size and lost his arm to save my grandson. Mark him well, and think of his courage! This man can ask anything of me!"

A knight pushed forward to look at Theodoric. "What is his name, Sire?"

Charles le Magne stared at Theodoric and laughed. "Yes, we must know your name."

The court became very silent as they all waited for Theodoric's answer. He was seized with fear and tried to speak, but could not. As he opened and closed his mouth, a woman came to the edge of his pallet and stared down at him, and then screamed in rage. She began to sob hysterically and had to be supported by another woman. She pointed at him again and said, "He is a thief! Because of him, my father is dead! He stole my father's purse, and thus our men were caught off guard when the Northmen came to kill them. Look! Look for my father's purse at his belt!"

Theodoric gazed at the woman in shock. It was the merchant's daughter. She and the foot soldier must have escaped through the woods to the Emperor's court. He wanted to cover his ears against her screams, but could not. One of the women took her to a corner of the room and helped her sit down, where she gradually grew quieter.

A gaunt and homely man came up to Theodoric and bent down to look at him more closely. He was not a pleasant man, and with despair, Theodoric recognized him. He was the same man who had ordered Theodoric to the dungeons to be tortured. The man lifted the edge of Theodoric's tunic and untied the merchant's fat purse with a satisfied smile. Standing, he handed it to the Emperor. "It is indeed true, Your Majesty. This is the same rogue that I placed in Your Majesty's dungeon years ago. He escaped, but now I have found him again."

Theodoric stared at the ceiling, unable to look at anyone. The thickening, uneasy silence was broken by Nithard.

"Grandfather."

King Charles looked down at the boy, who was tugging at his sleeve. "Yes, Nithard?"

Nithard looked around at the court, at the knights and ladies with their expressions of curiosity and faint hostility, and took a deep breath.

"He was running from the Northmen and came upon our camp in the forest, the day before Bero died. He admitted that he was a thief, but Bero trusted him and asked him to bring me through the woods to the court. At first, he said no, because he was afraid of coming here. But then, when Bero died, he told me that he would help me.

"He stayed with me, and when we came upon the Northmen, he did not run away. He encouraged me to avoid the battle and come directly to the court because he said that you would not want me killed. But when I insisted, he led me forward through the trees to the battle, and then he saved me.

"His name is Theodoric. His father was Theodoric, the storyteller, and his mother was a village woman named Chlotilde."

Nithard paused and looked at Theodoric. "I owe him my life, Grandfather."

King Charles was a fair man and a forward-thinking man. In battle, he had sometimes been brutal, but no more cruel than the standard of his times. It was a violent and barbaric age, but as a Christian, he had devoted himself to increasing his people's knowledge. He loved his sons and daughters and kept his daughters close to him, so close, in fact, that he would not permit them to marry. Instead, he allowed his daughters to take lovers and then recognized their illegitimate offspring and raised them at court. Nithard was such a child. It was thus that he listened to his grandson with more than the cursory attention generally given to children.

It was also perhaps that he was almost seventy years of age and had grown weary of killing. No one ever knew what went through his mind that day, except for his simple statement as he gazed down at the thief lying on the pallet.

"This man saved my grandson, and I am in his debt. He will be an honored servant to Nithard from this day hence."

◅§ ◅§ ◅§

Many weeks later, Nithard came upon Theodoric, sitting on a stone wall in the gardens of the Emperor. It was a beautiful morning, and a mockingbird was warbling and singing in the shrubbery. Theodoric's arm had healed, although he still felt unused to the empty sleeve below his elbow. He kept trying to use his left hand and kept rediscovering that it was no longer part of his body. It was very disconcerting since he had made use of both his hands with speed and agility since he had been a child. But his thieving days were now over. He consoled himself with the fact that at least it wasn't his right arm that had been cut off by the Northman.

Nithard looked at his empty sleeve with a sympathetic eye and carefully sat down on Theodoric's right side. He handed Theodoric a plum, and they proceeded to sit on the wall and spill plum juice down their chins onto their tunics. They were large and juicy plums, grown in his grandfather's gardens. Nithard and Theodoric didn't speak, but just sat and watched the dragonflies buzz across the sunflowers.

They sat and swung their short legs off the stone wall and basked in the morning sunlight. Nithard smiled at Theodoric and then belched, quite loudly.

Theodoric, in his new position as a loyal servant, decided that he must help his brave and noble master. His belch was much louder, and his grin was much larger. He had not told Nithard that long ago he had been a champion belcher in his village. Nithard, being the grandson of Charlemagne, never backed down from a challenge, even from a man who had saved his life.

The garden was soon filled with the sounds of belching, forever corrupting the Emperor's favorite mockingbird.

Later, when the mockingbird's belching sounds were brought to Charles' attention, he laughed with a very loud "Ha!" and belched a great and most magnificent belch.

No one ever beat the Emperor at anything.

Stories You Can Read
to Your Children

The Journey of Anhad

When the sun is especially hot in India, as it often is during the summer, taking a nap under a tree is an inviting prospect. When the chair placed under that broad-leafed tree is soft and comfortable, it is a foregone conclusion that sleep is the only proper way to spend one's afternoon. It seemed thus to Anhad that day, particularly because he had spent the entire morning helping his mother clean the house.

How much dust can one sweep up from nooks and corners? Anhad had wanted to grumble but had decided against it since his mother had promised him a very large slice of cake if he did an excellent job. When one is seven, cake is important. So he swept and dusted and straightened things until he was quite exhausted. Of course, he still had enough energy to eat cake. One never gets too tired for that, especially when the cake is chocolate.

With his last bite, he stood, preparing to burrow into the beckoning chair under the tree. His mother stopped him for a moment and asked, "Did you forget something?"

"Thank you for the cake, Mummy," he replied. His mother smiled, which made Anhad feel very pleased with himself. He liked it when she smiled, which of course she did quite a lot.

The chair was large, and as Anhad scrunched down into it and closed his eyes, the world around him felt far away. The sound of car horns faded, and even the cackle of the birds in the tree grew softer and more melodious. Sleep hugged him, and he sighed a huge sigh, a sigh of chocolate cake contentment and chores well done.

It might have been the cake, or perhaps the beauty of the tree that waved at him as he slept, but on that particular day, Anhad began to dream, a dream unlike any other. It started out with a jumble, much like his room when it was messy. Images of Pokémon, Ninja Turtles, and Power Rangers floated through his mind like lily pads, each one waving at him, saying, "Pick me! Pick me!"

Those images soon faded, however, and Anhad discovered that he was walking, far from home, along a winding dirt road at the foot of an enormous mountain. The landscape was unfamiliar, and there were no houses in sight. Just a road, with a mountain on the right, and dusty fields on the left, spotted with trees. He walked for a while and thought to himself that it was quite strange, and not as comfortable as sleeping in the chair in his backyard, just a few feet from the kitchen where he could get a glass of water if he needed one.

Ah, water. With that thought, he realized that he was thirsty and looked around, wondering where he could get something to drink. To his astonishment, right there on the side of the road, where it had not been a moment before, a counter and a stool had appeared. Behind the counter stood a man—if it was indeed a man. He looked older than the mountain itself and had a beard that covered half the counter and stretched out onto the road.

He grinned at Anhad and waved at him. "Come, sit down and let me give you some of my special mango milkshake. You will like it very much."

Anhad felt rather cautious, but it was even hotter on the road than it was back at his house, so he decided to accept the man's invitation. He gingerly sat on the stool and picked up the glass of mango juice. At his first sip, he felt a rush of power flow from his head all the way to the soles of his feet.

He drank the entire glass as the man watched him with a smile. When he was done, he handed it back to the man and very loudly burped.

The man laughed and said, "You like it, Anhad?"

"You know my name?"

The man leaned on the counter and twirled an extremely impressive moustache. "I know almost everything about you. You are Anhad, which is an excellent name, as it means 'limitless.' Yes, it is a very special name."

Anhad didn't know what to say and just stared at the man until the man laughed again and patted his shoulder. Motioning up the road, the man said, "Be careful as you go."

Anhad nodded and clambered off the stool. He glanced up the road for a moment and then turned to thank the old man, but the man and the counter were gone. There was not even a scuff mark in the dirt where the counter had been.

He felt confused, but the mango milkshake had been excellent, and its effects were still rippling through his body. He felt light and did a little skip as he walked along the road. As he came to the top of a small rise, he reached a circle, with the road branching off to the left and right. There was a water fountain in the middle of the circle, splashing merrily into a granite pool.

A woman was slumped against the fountain, with her head bent forward. Anhad wasn't sure if she was sleeping, so he stepped to her right and approached the fountain, thinking that he would splash water on his face. Just as he reached out his hands to scoop up the water, she looked up at him.

"Young man, can you help me?" she asked. She raised one arm and pointed to the fields on his left. "I am tired, and my companions are not able to help me."

Anhad looked at the fields and saw that they were not empty, as he had thought. The fields were dotted with people, digging and weeding and walking back and forth with carts filled with grain. As they walked, they made a strange clanking sound that he didn't recognize.

"Young man, can you help me?" The woman was tugging at his arm. He looked down at her again and saw that she was very old, with dirt and sweat streaking her face. He was about to speak, but suddenly he heard a horn blowing a mighty note, and then another and another.

Surprised, he wheeled around and saw a man striding down the road from the right. He held in his hand an ornate, golden trumpet. The man waved at him and blew his horn again as he reached the circle.

"Anhad! Anhad the Limitless! I am so happy to see you!"

The man strode up to Anhad and lifted him up and twirled him around, exclaiming all the while. He put Anhad down and looked at him with a huge grin.

"You are such a lucky young man!"

"I am?" Anhad felt very confused. The man was exceedingly and fantastically bright, so bright that Anhad's eyes hurt to look at him. He squinted and was able to see the man a bit better. The man was tall and was dressed in a long sherwani coat and trousers made entirely of finely woven gold. Even his shoes were gold.

Anhad didn't know what to say and simply gaped. The man laughed and took Anhad's hand. "I am the maharaja of this land, and you, my lucky, limitless boy, are in for the most amazing treat! Come, my palace is right over there." He pointed up the road to the right, to an enormous castle at the foot of the mountain.

Anhad couldn't think of a single thing to say, so he let the man lead him toward the palace. He didn't notice the old woman watching them as they walked away from the fountain.

The palace was even bigger than he had thought, with steps so steep and long that the man finally had to lift Anhad up and put him on his back. They walked up and around and came to massive double doors of gold. As they walked through the doors, Anhad felt overwhelmed. Everything was gold: the floors and walls and ceilings and every bit of furniture. The Maharaja put him down and then took his arm as they walked to the front of the palace, to a large room. The building overlooked the plain below, and Anhad could see the fountain and the fields beyond. The workers were still scurrying back and forth, and he could hear echoes of the strange clanking sound that he had heard before. The old woman was still sitting in front of the fountain.

The Maharaja looked annoyed at the scene and proceeded to close all of the shutters, covering the windows until the room was quiet. Turning to Anhad, he clapped his hands and smiled.

"Dear boy, you are so amazingly lucky. You have arrived at the one place where you can live up to your name. You are a limitless young man, and that means that you can have unlimited amounts of gold! As much as you can carry into this room. Think of what you can do with that gold! Come, tell me what you like to do. Sports? Games? Television? What do you like the most?"

Anhad spied a chair and sat down in it with a plump.

"Do you have any mango milkshakes? I'm very confused."

The Maharaja shook his head. "No, no mango milkshakes. But I have something better." He waved his hand, and a tall glass of golden liquid appeared on the table next to Anhad.

Anhad sipped it tentatively. He couldn't tell what it was, but it was cool, so he drank it.

Settling back into the chair, he looked around the room. Except for the chair and the table, the room was completely empty. The ceiling was high, and when Anhad snapped his fingers, there was a bit of an echo. He looked at the Maharaja and tried to think. The Maharaja stood quietly, with a smile playing across his face. Anhad suddenly realized that the man's eyes were gold.

"What do you mean when you say 'limitless?'" Anhad asked. "I don't understand. I'm only seven."

The Maharaja laughed. His laugh bounced against the walls, creating waves in the air. "You are limitless because you can get whatever you want. You can have all the gold and wealth that you want, and with that gold, you can buy anything. It doesn't matter that you are seven. You will grow and become powerful and famous because of your gold."

Anhad wrinkled his brow. "But why me?"

"Because of your name! And it is my purpose to show little boys like you that they can have anything they want. Riches beyond imagination!"

The Maharaja held out his hand. "Come, let me show you what you have to do."

Anhad stood up and took the Maharaja's hand. They walked from the room, down a long hallway, and arrived at a huge hall, filled from floor to ceiling with gold bricks. The Maharaja picked up a brick and gave it to Anhad.

"You must come to this room and carry as many bricks as you can, back to the room from whence we came. In that room, you must build a playhouse from these bricks, and make it as high and broad as you like. With every brick, your power to be limitless will grow and grow, and you will fulfill your destiny."

The Maharaja picked up a few bricks and said, "Here, let me help you with the first bricks."

They went back to the front room, and the Maharaja showed Anhad how to put the bricks together to make a wall.

"How will I make the roof?" Anhad asked.

The Maharaja winked and said, "The roof is special. When your walls are complete, just say, 'Roof!' and it will be there."

The Maharaja stood up and stared at Anhad. "Just remember, with every new brick, you will become happier and happier to see so many bricks. You will be a success! You will be limitless indeed."

He walked to the door and turned and said, "I will see you when your house is built."

A moment later, he was gone, and Anhad stood in the middle of the room and stared at the bricks stacked on the floor. He found their yellow glint and shimmer fascinating and exciting. His mummy had said that he could be limitless, and now it seemed that it would be true. He must make the wall as high as he possibly could.

As Anhad trudged back and forth between the brick room and his new playhouse, he daydreamed and thought about all the things he could buy with so much gold. He tried keeping count of the bricks but got lost somewhere around four-hundred and thirty-seven. He decided to make a very large playhouse, with rooms inside it, and doorways and windows. He made piles of gold bricks to sit on and created makeshift tables. His focus grew intense, and he forgot everything except the golden bricks that he carried and laid out so carefully. He had no idea how much time was passing.

As his house grew, he noticed that his breathing was becoming labored, and he was feeling slightly dizzy. He walked by a mirror in the hallway and wondered at first who was in the mirror. The face staring back at him was drained of color, and his eyes had deep shadows around them. It frightened him, so he quickly moved away, carrying his bricks to the front room.

The air in the front room had grown stuffy and close, and the light had faded until all he could see was the shimmering house growing ever larger in the middle of the room. It was a beautiful and mesmerizing sight, and it brought Anhad immense pride to look upon it. He felt that he could sit and gaze at it forever.

As he stepped up to the house to place a golden brick on a new outcrop of wall, he lost his balance and, with a bang, dropped the brick on his big toe. The pain was excruciating, and he wondered if he was going to faint. He fell to his knees, with his forehead against a golden wall, and closed his eyes for a moment. He was exhausted and was surprised that he felt so because the house really was beautiful.

Slumped there against the wall, with his eyes shut tight, he felt like he was twirling around and around in a deep, black void. He began to feel frightened and struggled against the blackness. He suddenly felt intensely lonely. It was then that he heard a very tiny whisper in his mind. He didn't know if it was his thoughts or a person's voice, but the words were insistent: "Go outside! Quick! Go outside!"

Anhad opened his eyes and, with great effort, stumbled to his feet, and weaved his way out of the front room, down the long hallways, to the entrance of the palace. As he stepped through the golden doors, the whisper came again: "Go down the steps to the road! Quick! Run! Run down the steps to the road!"

He didn't know how he did it, but as he ran down the steps, his feet began to slide from step to step, only touching the edges, as if he was skiing. He was quite surprised, but relieved, because it was a very long set of steps, and he felt weakened to his bones. His feet seemed to take over, and as he glided down the long descent of steps, the whisper came again, and said, "Sliding over the steps like this is called glemmering. Do you like it?"

He nodded and shouted, "Yes!" And then he was at the bottom of the steps, standing on the road. The whisper said, "Run now, to the fountain!"

He ran, and arrived at the fountain, and threw himself into the pool of water and rolled back and forth. After splashing and hollering and dunking his head in the cool water, he climbed out and leaned against the edge. The sun was still shining, but when he looked to his left, the steps and the palace were gone. Only the mountain stood there, lifting high into the sky.

He shook his head, wiping the water from his face, completely confused. Something tugged at his leg, and he turned to see the old woman sitting there, slumped against the fountain, looking up at him piteously.

"Young man, can you help me?"

To Anhad, at that moment, the old woman looked very forlorn, and he felt a pang that he had not helped her before. Crouching down in front of her, he gazed at her and said, "What can I do?"

The woman sat up straighter and pointed at the fields.

"Listen," she said.

Anhad looked at the fields and saw that the workers were still there, digging and weeding and pushing their carts. He listened and once again heard a strange clanking sound.

Looking at the old woman, he asked, "What is it?"

"Help me get up," the woman replied.

He took her arms and helped her stand. She was taller than he thought, but she was hunched over in a horrible, upside-down "L" shape. She waved toward the field and said, "Help me go to the field, and I will show you."

They walked slowly along the road to the edge of the field where some workers were on their knees, digging in the earth with trowels. The workers looked up as they approached but then turned their faces away as if they were afraid.

The old woman walked to a girl bent over a stone in the ground. She was trying as hard as she could to dig the rock out of the earth, but it wouldn't budge. Her face was covered with dirt, and tears were rolling down her cheeks. The old woman sat next to the girl and gently moved the hem of the girl's sari away from her ankles. Attached to both ankles were large shackles, with an iron chain between them.

The girl was embarrassed and quickly pulled her sari over her ankles, turning her head away.

The old woman looked up at Anhad. "Do you see, Anhad?"

Anhad nodded. "Yes." He raised his hands questioningly. "What can I do? And how do you know my name?"

The old woman slowly stood up and stared at him. "Everyone here knows your name. Anhad, the Limitless Boy." She motioned around the field at the other workers. "What do you think you should do?"

Anhad rubbed his brow. He felt very much better than he had in the palace, but he still felt a weakness in his bones. He looked around the field and spied a white rock, about the size of a mango. Thinking about that, he realized that he would dearly love to have a mango milkshake, but something in him impelled him to ignore his thirst for the moment.

He picked up the white rock and, without knowing exactly why, walked to the girl, bent down, and asked, "May I?"

The girl nodded and pulled her sari away from her ankles, revealing the shackles and chain. Anhad raised the white rock high in the air and brought the rock down against each shackle in turn. As the rock hit the metal, sparks shot up from the blow, and the chains disappeared.

The girl stared at her ankles, unsure of what to do. She looked at the old woman, who nodded at her and smiled. Trembling and crying, the girl sat forward and hugged Anhad, squeezing him tightly, and said, "Thank you! Thank you! Thank you!"

Turning to the old woman, Anhad grinned. He felt very much better than he had in the palace. He was about to speak, but instead, he noticed that the old woman had her hand out toward him, holding a beautiful crystal goblet filled to the very top with mango milkshake.

He took the goblet from her and was about to take a sip when he glanced at the girl. The girl was staring at the cup as if she had never, ever seen a mango milkshake in her entire life. He ran his tongue across his lips, which suddenly felt like old, broken sandpaper, and with a rueful grin handed the goblet to the girl. Her eyes widened, and she seized the goblet and drank it down greedily.

Anhad gazed at her as she drank and felt a very peculiar warmth in his chest and something happening around his eyes. Wiping his eyes with his hand, he felt a tap on his shoulder. The old woman had her arm out again, with an even larger goblet of mango milkshake. Anhad laughed, all of a sudden, and drank the milkshake down in one go.

When he finished the drink, he stood up and looked around the field and then down at the old woman. Holding up the white rock, he nodded toward the workers.

"I guess I should go to them, too?"

"Of course," said the woman.

Anhad went from person to person, across field after field. There were old men and young, girls and mothers, and even a baby, with tiny little shackles between its feet. The workers were unkempt and afraid at first, as Anhad approached them. But as he broke their chains with the white rock, the others began to notice what was happening and looked at Anhad with eagerness as he approached.

They all hugged him when their shackles disappeared—every single one, except the baby, who just smiled at Anhad and said something in the strange language that all babies know well. Anhad had never been hugged so much in his entire life of seven years—not even on holidays or birthdays with his aunties all around him. He had to admit that their hugs felt exceedingly wonderful.

At the end of one of the fields, when the last worker had hugged him and run to her friends, he looked around for the old woman. She was standing right behind him, which caused him to jump back slightly in surprise. Even more astonishing to Anhad was that she was no longer old.

Her face was the same, sort of, with wise, old eyes, but her skin was smooth, and she was standing straight, regally, and was dressed in a beautiful emerald-colored sari. She smiled at him and took both of his hands in hers and squeezed them affectionately.

"Well done, Anhad," she said.

He felt embarrassed and blushed.

She pointed at the mountain and said, "Let's go to the top, shall we?"

Before he could say a word, she jumped into the air, holding his hands and pulling him with her. They flew—yes, flew—to the top of the mountain as fast as any bird could have done, and perhaps faster than that.

The mountaintop was far above the fields. Anhad had not realized how tall it was, but it seemed even higher than Mount Kangchenjunga, even though it was green, with beautiful flowers and trees at the top. There was no snow, and it was warm, with butterflies flitting around their heads.

They landed on a grassy knoll and stood for a moment, looking at the fields and road below. Anhad was astonished that he could see the people in the field as clearly as if he was looking through a telescope. He could even see the baby, kicking its legs in delight. Anhad thought about how he was feeling and couldn't put his finger on it. It was like the warm feelings he had when all of his aunties hugged him one after the other.

The old woman, who was no longer old, sat down in a chair that had suddenly appeared, and put her arm around him and squeezed him against her and smiled at him. She waved her hand, and a chair appeared behind him, in which he obligingly sat. They sat together for a while, without speaking, watching the birds fly by until the woman raised her hands and motioned toward the sky.

The sky directly above the mountain grew dark, and the stars appeared. The moon floated into view and sat at the edge of the circle of night sky, gazing down at them.

The woman looked at Anhad. "You've had quite a day, haven't you?"

Anhad stared at her. "I guess so."

She pinched his cheek, amused at his reaction. "You met the Maharaja. He's a sly one, isn't he? But he's the voice of the cold and the dark—the voice of loneliness. I'm glad you escaped his clutches."

Anhad was silent, not wanting to think about the Maharaja. The woman rubbed his shoulder sympathetically.

"He said that you are limitless, and you are. You absolutely are. And today you discovered what that means. To be limitless means that you are alive and growing and expanding, and today you discovered the great secret of life: that only loving thoughts and actions are truly infinite. Because love always creates more love."

"Oh," said Anhad.

She laughed and said, "I know this is hard to understand. You might not remember what I say, but then again, you might, because you are a special and intelligent boy."

She pointed up at the sky. "See? Look at the stars, and remember the flowers and birds and butterflies and babies. Always remember babies. All of those things say one thing. The universe is made of love."

"That baby was really cute, wasn't he?" Anhad replied. "I still don't know what he said."

"Do you know why you felt sick in the Maharaja's palace?"

Anhad wrinkled his brow. "No, I don't. It was awful."

The woman turned to him and took his face in her hands and looked at him for a long time. Anhad thought that she was extraordinarily beautiful. Like a princess or a queen. He looked back at her and would have felt embarrassed, but her eyes were so soft and so warm that he simply felt safe.

"You felt sick because just thinking about gold is so small. Just thinking about yourself puts you in a prison. You have to think about other people if you want to be happy. Like you did in the field below."

She laughed. "But enough lessons for today. I have a much better idea."

She waved her hand, and there on his lap was a plate, with an enormous, very scrumptious-looking piece of chocolate cake.

Anhad looked at the cake and looked at the princess and saw that she was waving at him.

"Goodbye, dear Anhad. Just remember that you are loved."

As she spoke, her face looked far away, growing smaller and smaller, as if she was at the wrong end of a telescope. Her face finally became a dot and then disappeared altogether. Anhad felt confused and shifted in his chair. He couldn't see the stars or the mountain or the field and suddenly realized that his eyes were closed. He opened them, a little tentatively, not sure what he would see.

There above him was the broad-leafed tree in his backyard, and in front of him was his very own mummy, holding a lovely white plate with a particularly delicious-looking piece of chocolate cake.

"Anhad, you've been asleep for the longest time, so I thought you might like to eat the last piece of chocolate cake."

She handed him the cake, and of course—of course—he took it, since he was an obedient boy, and besides, who could turn down chocolate cake?

His mother watched him as he took a large forkful of cake and rolled his eyes in delight. She laughed and tousled his hair.

"You really are an extraordinary boy, aren't you, dear?"

Anhad didn't have any idea at that moment what he should say, so he said the only thing that a boy in his position could. He smiled very widely, with bits of chocolate cake stuck between his teeth, and said, not at all clearly because his mouth was quite full:

"Thank you, Mummy!"

Mock Bug's Escape:
The Incident of the Alien Child

It was the resounding thump of an alien child falling from the sky that woke Farmer Welton from his drunken slumber. He had wandered out of his farmhouse around noon, carrying a jug of liquor and some Oreos. Sitting there in the backyard, at an old beech-wood table, he had gorged himself until he had finally fallen asleep. Did he dream? We'll never know, but we do know that he drooled.

When the sound of the loud thump reached deep into the cobwebs of his brain, he grunted and snorted and sat upright so quickly that he fell off his chair. Glaring and growling, he stood, wiping the spittle from his beard. He didn't see anything unusual at first, but after rubbing his eyes a bit, he saw that the source of the thump was a small skinny child curled up under his clothesline.

Farmer Welton was not ordinarily a curious man. In fact, many of his neighbors had often wondered if he had much of a brain at all, although they did allow that he knew how to plant a row of corn. On this particular afternoon, he found himself impelled to lean over and nudge the child with the toe of his boot.

"Hey! You!" he asked. "What are you doin' in my yard?"

The child didn't move. In fact, as Farmer Welton leaned over him, he couldn't quite tell if the child was even breathing. The child was a very pale boy with extraordinary green hair that was sticking straight up from his head. Welton nudged him again and put his ear on the boy's chest to listen for a heartbeat. He had seen that done on one of those police shows and felt a twinge of pride that he had remembered such a thing. He couldn't hear a heartbeat, so he stood up and put his hands on his hips and spat. Much to his surprise, the child immediately sat up.

"Eeeeuuuu!" said the boy. "What is that awful smell!"

Welton jumped back slightly. "What smell?" he asked.

The boy stood up and brushed himself off. His face was more than pale; it was a solid white, like the side of Farmer Welton's chicken coop before the chickens had done a job on the paint. He had a large blue circle on his forehead, and earrings dangling from his ears. One ear was blue, and the other was red. All in all, he presented such a bizarre appearance that Farmer Welton didn't know what to say. Opening and closing his mouth a few times, he let out a nervous hiss and said the only thing he could think of.

"Are you from New York City?"

The boy glared at Welton with the utter scorn that some children are masters of, and said, "I am not! My name is Mock Bug, and I am from the planet Nocks in the Chukbok system."

"Oh." It wasn't much of an answer, but Welton really couldn't think of much else. He stared at the boy, and Mock Bug stared back until a dog barked down by the barn. The sound made the boy jump and run behind a bush.

"You've got to save me! He's after me!" he wailed.

Farmer Welton shook his head. "That's just old Rat, my dog. He won't hurt you."

"No, not him!" Mock Bug put his arms over his head. "Ik Monk is after me. He's mean and nasty and horrible! He's been chasing me for days and days!"

Farmer Welton wrinkled his brow and tried to understand. The weird names were giving him indigestion. Rubbing his stomach, he did what any man in his position would do. He strode manfully over to the table and picked up the jug and took an impressively large swig. He knew he had done the right thing because he felt better right away. Holding out the package of Oreos, he asked, "You want some?"

Mock Bug peered out from under his arms and nodded. Without so much as a by-your-leave, there was a faint pop in the air and the boy was standing right in front of Welton. The farmer jumped slightly and took another swig from his jug.

"How the heck did you do that?" he asked.

"Do what?" Mock Bug asked, reaching for a cookie.

"That!" Welton said. "That moving over here without walking thing."

Mock Bug didn't answer for a moment, as he was busy shoving Oreos into his mouth. "That's how we move around on our planet. Don't you do that too?"

"No!" said Welton. "We walk with our legs, the way the Good Lord made us."

Mock Bug reached for the jug, but Farmer Welton held it away from him. "That's not for you, my boy."

With a pop and a pop and a pop, Mock Bug was in the tree, then on top of the shed, and then in front of the farmer again, who rubbed his eyes and took another swig from his jug.

Mock Bug stamped his foot angrily. "Are you going to help protect me or not!"

Farmer Welton sat down and thought for a moment. "Seems like you don't need much help with all your popping here and popping there."

The boy looked around fearfully. "Ik Monk is much faster than me. He's chased me all over your world. I got away from him at Disney World. I'm trying to get to the Air and Space Museum, but he's coming, I can feel it!"

Welton rubbed his chin reflectively. "I don't rightly know what I can do. You think he'll come here?"

Mock Bug started to answer but stopped when he heard barking. It was the farmer's dog, Rat, barking furiously, straining against his leash by the edge of the barn. Farmer Welton and the boy stood up and stared at the dog. "What's got into that dog," Welton muttered.

"Look!" shrieked Mock Bug. "It's him!"

Farmer Welton stared where the boy was pointing. Sure enough, there was a man in dark clothing coming toward them across the field. The man didn't seem to be walking as much as appearing, from spot to spot, getting closer and closer. Mock Bug ran to the farmer's side and clutched his hand and hid behind him.

"It is Ik Monk! Please don't let him get me! Please!"

Welton looked back toward the house. "I think I should get my gun."

Before he could take a step, however, the stranger was in the yard, striding toward Mock Bug.

"Mock Bug!" he shouted. "Stay where you are!" The man leveled a bright red stick at Mock Bug, and a loud humming was heard. Mock Bug suddenly sat down in a heap and started to sob.

Farmer Welton hitched up his trousers and stepped forward pugnaciously. "Now, see here, Mister. I'm not going to let you hurt this boy!"

The man stared at Welton. He was dressed entirely in black and had jet-black hair that stuck up like a porcupine. His face was white, and he had three bright green stripes on his forehead. His chin was colored blue, and he had round dots across his upper lip where his mustache might have been. He looked young, which puzzled the farmer. Welton was sure he must be a city feller because his voice and accent were most peculiar. He spoke in a staccato, clipped fashion, but with a singsong whine. He suddenly let out a long, discordant, maniacal laugh.

"Hurt Mock Bug! Ha! He must come with me now. Mock Bug, come now!"

With that, he held out his long red stick and pointed it at the boy, who cowered behind the farmer. Welton stood forward with his chest out and shoulders back and said, "Over my dead body!"

Ik Monk sneered at the farmer and said, "Dead bodies are my speciality. Nothing will prevent me from taking Mock Bug back with me." He straightened up and swept his hand toward the sky in a grand, expressive gesture. "I will die, if I have to, to bring Mock Bug back to the people of Nocks."

Mock Bug whimpered and clutched the farmer's leg. "I'm not going back! I'm not!"

Ik Monk scowled at Mock Bug, so naturally, Farmer Welton glared at Ik Monk. Mock Bug hadn't had much experience scowling or glaring, so he cried, which is what alien children do in every corner of the universe except the BokBu system, but that's not their fault.

It appeared that they were in a standoff. The dog barked, but no one moved.

In this scene of tension and tribulation, Farmer Welton tried real hard to think about what would happen next. His gun was far out of reach. He considered tackling Ik Monk, but he wasn't sure what that contraption of a red stick would do. He yearned for another sip from his jug, or even an Oreo, but he was afraid to move and break the spell.

Just as Farmer Welton's legs started to tremble from the stress, he heard a long siren-like sound. There was a flash of light and a loud bang, and there in the middle of his back yard stood a female alien. She was dressed in a strange boxlike garment with her head coming out of the top. Her hair was piled high on her head, with twigs and branches and sparkly things stuck in her hair. Her face was as white as the others, and she had large blue circles around her eyes and mouth. On the tip of her nose, she had a shiny red spot. Both ears were bright green. Farmer Welton forgot all about Ik Monk for a moment as he gazed in astonishment at this most unusual lady. The woman ignored him and pointed her finger at Ik Monk.

"Ik Monk!" she said. "I am very disappointed in you."

"My queen!" he replied. "Forgive me!" With that, Ik Monk knelt on the ground and proceeded to bang his head against the earth over and over again.

Queen? Farmer Welton felt very confused. The only queen he had ever heard of was the Queen of England, and this lady didn't sound like her at all. No, sir, not even a little bit. She spoke in a high, shrill whine that was off-key and sounded like angry hogs fighting with a flock of chickens, with neither side winning.

Ik Monk turned his head briefly toward the farmer and hissed, "It is Queen Smirk Bug! You must bow down to her now, or she will be very, very angry."

"Awww, phooey," answered Farmer Welton. "I ain't bowin' down to nobody, queen or no queen. I'm an American. And what is it with these weirdo names, anyway? What kind of planet do you guys come from?"

Queen Smirk Bug let out a pop and suddenly stood nose to nose with Farmer Welton. She was rather imposing, although she looked far too young to be a queen. He stared back her, as bravely as he could.

"Our names mean different things in our language," she said. "Your language is far stranger than ours. Smirk means 'Most High and Beautiful Exalted One.' Bug is our family name, and means 'The Most Intelligent and Capable Leaders in the Universe.' Do you have any other questions, silly man?"

Farmer Welton gulped but forged ahead. "Well, how come you look so young, and that guy Ik Monk, or whatever he's called, looks so young? You look like teenagers. That's kinda weird, ain't it?"

The Queen suddenly smiled and let out a pealing laugh and popped all over the yard. Hanging upside down from the clothesline bar, she laughed and said, "Young! He has called me young! Oh, joy! We must record it for all on our planet to hear!" She let out a laugh and a pop and was suddenly back in front of the farmer.

"I am seven hundred years old, my good man. Compared to most of my subjects, I look old indeed. Take Ik Monk there. He is at least three hundred. I must thank you for such a compliment." She let out another raucous laugh. "And we don't even use plastic surgeons as you do on this planet! Oh, joy, oh joy!"

Farmer Welton was very confused. He walked over to the table and took a long slug from his jug until it was empty. He banged on the bottom, trying to coax a few more drops out of it, and then hurled the pitcher across the lawn in disgust. Turning to Mock Bug, who was sitting in a heap on the ground, he asked, "And him? How old is he?"

The Queen held out her hand to Mock Bug, who cowered and shrank away. With a sigh, she said, "My son is going to be forty-five in three days. That's why we have come to bring him back to Nocks for his coronation and his birthday."

"I won't go!! I won't!" howled Mock Bug.

The Queen frowned and pointed her finger at Ik Monk, who banged his head on the ground again. "Ik Monk! If you hadn't let him get away from you at Disney World, I wouldn't have had to interrupt my sunbathing back on Nocks! My left shoulder was almost tan! I only let you bring him to Earth for a vacation because you said you could take care of him!"

Ik Monk started to cry, and crawled forward and grasped the hem of the Queen's dress. "I'm so sorry, My Queen! You may take away all my privileges! You can lock me up! You can beat me with the husks of rotten wuuppuu plants! I am sorry, sorry, sorry, sorry!"

"Oh, get up," the Queen muttered. Ik Monk snuffled and stood up, hanging his head. The Queen turned to Mock Bug. "My child, you must come back with us now. The whole planet is gathering for your birthday, and your father has prepared a special gift for you."

Mock Bug reluctantly stood up and said, "What kind of gift, Mumu? A Nockanese flying car? A blue one, maybe?"

The Queen winked at Farmer Welton. "I won't say blue, but it looked like it might fly."

Farmer Welton felt very bewildered indeed as the Queen gathered Mock Bug to her side and took the hand of the repentant Ik Monk. She winked once again at the farmer and said, "Of course, my dear sir, no one on Earth will believe a word of it if you try to tell people about our visit today. I would recommend that you keep it to yourself."

The farmer nodded and watched as the three of them raised their hands toward the sky. With a loud pop and a whistle, they were gone. Rat barked once, as if to say good-bye.

Farmer Welton walked to his old beechwood table and sat down heavily. His jug was lying empty on the grass, and the Oreos were eaten. He thought it must have been a dream, perhaps brought on by too much drinking.

"I've got to get back on the wagon," he muttered. "I'm goin' nuts." He stood up and turned to walk into his house. Something on the ground glinted at him in the sunlight. With a grunt, he bent over and picked up the object. It was one of Mock Bug's earrings. Holding the earring in his hand, he turned it over and over. With a loud laugh, he clutched it in his hand and raised his fist to the sky and shouted, "I saw you, Mock Bug! I really did! I'm not crazy!"

Then the farmer did something that would have convinced his neighbors that he was crazy after all, if they had seen him. He danced in his yard, round and round, in a clumsy jig, shouting, "Happy Birthday, Mock Bug! Happy Birthday to you! Happy Birthday, Mock Bug!"

Mock Bug, who was sipping Lanlu juice and yawning, turned to his mother the Queen and said, "Can you hear the funny man, Mumu?"

"Yes, my sweet," the Queen replied. "You can visit him again next year if you like. Go to sleep now, there's a good boy."

With a smile and a sigh, Mock Bug curled up on the sofa of the Royal Spacecraft and dreamed of blue Nockanese flying cars and a dancing farmer far below.

The Sad Tale of Rupert and Eggbert

*R*upert was a peaceful cat.

He lay in the sun all day, dreaming of nice things that walked on four legs.

He was a playful cat.

One day, a small, timid mouse named Eggbert danced across Rupert's nose. But Rupert wasn't upset at all. No, not at all.

He lay there calmly, wondering why Eggbert had two g's in his name. He wondered if the mouse had a brother named Bacon.

Eggbert was a merry fellow. He danced and played and frolicked around Rupert for quite a long time—a long time, that is, for a mouse. He twirled his tiny whiskers and danced and danced, thinking all the while about New York Cheddar.

Rupert was glad that Eggbert had come to see him. He didn't mind the dancing—at least not for a little while.

After a bit, Rupert gazed out of the window and thought of nice things that walked on four legs.

He yawned and smiled, rather sleepily.

When Rupert glanced away from the window, Eggbert was nowhere to be seen.

But Rupert didn't mind at all.

No, not at all, for Rupert's tummy was now full.

The Bird That Was Saved
by a THING

It was a Tuesday when it Happened. The baby sparrow, affectionately called Lewie by his father and mother (short for Llewellyn, of course), had decided that today was the Day when he could fly. His mother, Frances, had looked at him severely and cuffed him with the tip of her left wing.

"Fly? At your age? I don't think so!"

Lewie, unfortunately, wasn't known around the neighborhood for being terribly swift. The mourning doves had delicately suggested to Frances that perhaps Lewie wasn't a sparrow at all. His chirps were a bit off-key, you see, and that annoyed the mourning doves immensely.

Lewie's mother had always defended him, for even though Lewie was extremely shortsighted and a tiny bit stupid, he was her boy. Mothers are like that.

So, when Lewie looked up at her, quite blithely ignoring her cuff, and said once again, "But, Mother, today *is* the day! I just know that I can fly today!" she gulped and idly considered putting him up for adoption.

"No is no, young man. 'Nuff said."

With that, she turned her back and continued with the happy task of regurgitating worms for Lewie's siblings. Frances had forgotten the cardinal rule for all bird mothers—never turn your back on a flighty child.

She can be forgiven, frankly, for the worms were particularly chewy that day, and she had to work extra hard. Lewie's father, Gilbert, was also quite an interruption. He kept nudging her with his wing and muttering something about "sparrows on a telephone wire." She simply clucked and crossly told him to be romantic *after* lunch.

Can you imagine her shock when she turned around to feed Lewie and found him entirely gone? (Gone missing, that is, as the English would say.) Oh, the noise that Frances made that horrible Tuesday, at noon! Soon dozens of neighbors were perched all around, giving advice of all sorts, most of it bad, but still well-intentioned.

"Have you looked on the roof? Or under the nest? What was his name again? Was it a fox?"

The fox remark was enough for Frances. She became, she turned into, she transmogrified into that most fearsome of creatures—a mother on a rampage. Sticking out her beak, she ran and hopped and flew from branch to branch until, quite exhausted by her effort, she landed on the roof of the Big House. She couldn't imagine how Lewie might have gotten as far as the Big House—she had told him and told him to stay away from that awful place where the Cat lived—but you know how children are . . .

Frances fearfully peered over the edge of the roof, half expecting to see the slinking, white shadow of the Cat running through the garden with poor Lewie in its murderous maw. What a sigh of relief she breathed when she saw absolutely nothing moving in the yard below. No cat. No broken and pitiful bones. Oh, the trials a mother must go through!

Imagine her astonishment when she heard a chirp—in fact, quite a series of very loud, rather hysterical chirps—coming from the telephone wire running under the eaves of the house. There on the wire was her errant son Lewie, flapping his tiny wings and raising his quivering beak toward the sky as if to bleat, "Momma, where are you?"

Frances almost swallowed the bit of worm that was still stuck to her beak but instead tried to wring her claws in dismay.

"Lewie! Up here! What are you doing on that telephone wire?"

"Oh, Mother! 'Tis you! You've come to save me!"

If sparrows could growl, Frances surely would have. But instead, she squawked.

"Save you! I'm going to spank you with both of my wings, you naughty boy! Why are you sitting on that wire, and *why* are you facing the wall? Come up here at once, and let's go home!"

There was a long pause. A very long pause. Frances wondered if perhaps the Cat had been successful after all and had made a large dent in Lewie's tiny tongue. Suddenly, she heard a cough—an apologetic, polite little cough. She leaned perilously over the edge, cocking her head as mother sparrows often do, and focused one of her eyes on Lewie.

"Did you say something, Lewie?"

Lewie shifted uncomfortably and coughed again, peering up at his Mother from under one wing.

"Mother, I quite hate to say it, but I'm stuck."

"Stuck?"

"Yes, Mother. I knew I could fly today." Lewie's chest swelled and puffed with pride. "Today really *was* the day! I flew!" Then, his head drooped once more, and he mumbled so quietly that Frances hardly heard him. "There's just one problem."

"Yes?" Frances focused her other eye on Lewie, who seemed to grow smaller as he tried to hide under his wing.

"I'm so close to this wall that I can't turn around!"

The hardened bit of worm suddenly did travel down Frances' gullet, as she gulped in quite an unladylike manner. Raising her head to the sky, she flapped her wings and let out an amazingly long series of chirps. If a postman had been near the house, he would have thought it was an invasion. But it was just a Mother.

Her frantic chirping roused her husband, Gilbert, from his nap. (He would *not* have been napping at a time like this, but he had been up all night scouting for new worm patches.) Soon the rooftop and neighboring branches were crowded with their relatives and friends, all once again offering advice that was not useful at all.

"Look, Harold, he's stuck against the wall" and . . . "My oh my, Mildred, look at poor little Lewie. He can't turn around. How on earth did he get stuck against the wall?" and . . . "At least it wasn't a fox!"

Frances leaned over and glared at Lewie.

"Lewie, how *could* you do this?"

Lewie's head feathers shook with tiny sparrow sobs. "I'm sorry, Mother. I really am."

Frances gazed to her left, and gazed to her right, and then stared up at the sky. She felt rather faint and considered expiring, but just as she raised her wing in despair, she glanced toward the ground. And stopped.

There was a Man-Thing moving through the garden. In fact, there was a congregation of People-Things, all grouped around the flowers, waving their wings at her Lewie. She had never been able to figure out what these People-Things were: Their wings were very strange, entirely without feathers, and they never seemed to leave the ground. She *was* certain that they weren't *cats*. At least, she didn't think so, because she had never seen one eat a sparrow. Her uncle Clarence had told her once that they had many names: Men, or People, or even Lady, and, once in a while, "Mrs. Buckingham."

Frances sat and watched as one of the smaller persons chirped at a Lady-Person. The Lady went into the Big House and soon came out with an even bigger Man-Thing, holding the Man's wing. Gilbert flew down and perched next to Frances, and looked very grave—standard practice for sparrow fathers.

"Doesn't look good, Frances. Looks bad. Very bad."

Frances privately agreed and stared as the large Man-Thing bent over and put something on its feet. She could tell they were feet because the Man-Thing walked on them—although they seemed awfully imbalanced without an opposing claw.

She nudged Gilbert and pointed as two of the smaller persons came hopping around the corner of the Big House, carrying a long ladder between them. Gilbert looked at Lewie sympathetically (who was by this time way past the point of sparrow hysteria) and sighed, as if to say, "Son, say your prayers."

Suddenly there was a great clamor and rattle, and a series of horrible scraping sounds as the Man-Thing placed the ladder against the wall of the Big House, right next to Lewie! Frances leaned against Gilbert, this time *really* feeling faint, and bleated out a tiny chirp.

"Lewie! We love you!"

Lewie folded his little wings and looked up at his neighbors and relatives who were lining the tree branches. They were busily composing poetic farewells, already speaking about Lewie in the past tense (a bad sign indeed). Staring at them, with a trembling beak, he let out one final, forlorn chirp.

"Bye."

You see, Lewie had two problems. Not only was his tiny beak firmly facing the wall, but he was also suffering from Lack of Knowledge. Frances had never expected him to fly—not on this particular Tuesday—so she hadn't yet bothered to tell him about Men, or Ladies, or little Child-Things—and certainly *not* about Mr. and Mrs. Buckingham. All Lewie knew was that there were some terribly large things in the garden below—and one of them was coming his way.

Lewie gazed down at the enormous THING that had no feathers on its shiny head and watched in resignation and horror as it slowly climbed up the strange metal tree branch toward him. The Thing climbed slowly, and came closer and closer and closer and closer and opened its wing feathers and came closer and closer and closer and then *closed* its wing feathers around Lewie's trembling body and Lewie just felt like SCREAMING—but couldn't because sparrow babies aren't very good at screaming.

So he chirped. And promptly fainted.

Lewie came to, with a start, and realized, in a vague, dreamy kind of way, that the monstrous THING was climbing back down the metal tree branch. Lewie struggled against its awful wing feathers—which didn't seem to be like any feathers he'd ever seen—but struggled to no avail. He was a prisoner of the THING.

His little sparrow chest heaved in despair as the Thing hopped onto the ground and triumphantly raised Lewie in the air, showing him to the smaller, noisy, horrid Things who clacked and crowed and chattered—a bit like blue jays, it seemed to Lewie.

Lewie began to feel quite seasick as the Thing walked through the grass and the flower garden, raising Lewie up in the air. The Thing kept looking up at the sky, circling around and around. Suddenly, the Thing stopped and pointed its wing toward the roof, where Frances and Gilbert were sitting, watching as if turned to stone.

Lewie heard the Thing chirp a very loud chirp—and then Lewie felt the Thing's wing feathers loosen around his body. He looked at the Thing, and the THING looked back at him! Lewie was free! Oh, the joy of a narrow escape!

Lewie began to puff his chest out with pride, already thinking of a dramatic sonnet he could recite to his cousin Myrna about his Great Adventure when he felt the THING's feathers shift against his body. Deciding quite practically that sonnets weren't that important, Lewie did what any good sparrow baby would do when faced with almost certain death at the wing of a THING. He gently, ever so gently, left a lovely white deposit on the wing of the THING and flew! Flew into the sky and was free!

"Mother! Where are you?"

Frances sprang from the rooftop and raced through the air and kissed Lewie, *smack*, right in the middle of the air of the yard, and said, "Lewie! You silly boy! Come home right now, and finish your lunch!"

Lewie smiled at his mother and chirped at his father and said, "Yes, Mother. Yes, Father. Thank you for saving me!"

As Frances flew to a nearby tree, she thought she heard one of the smaller Persons singing, as the huge Man stood there, shaking its wing feather. She couldn't have heard it singing, for all sparrows know that Person-Things can't carry a tune, but she really did think that she heard the smaller person sing, "The little birdie pooped on my daddy. . . . Oh, the little birdie pooped on my daddy. . . ."

Frances clucked and looked at Lewie. "Lewie, you didn't. . . ."

Lewie just grinned, with a bit of worm sticking out of his beak, and began to sing a song about The Great Adventure that happened on a Tuesday, during Lunch—the day that he Flew and was saved by a THING.

Yes, indeed, the Man-Thing with no feathers on its head saved
the wee sparrow perched on the wire, facing the wall.
The grand event was immortalized in the song
"The Little Birdie Pooped On My Daddy."

The Other Toe Day

A short play for young children in one act

Cast of Characters

BOY: A baby boy, residing in his mummy's tummy

UNCLE RUDOLPHO: Boy's great, great, great-granduncle, the boy's travel guide

TUMMY ANGEL: A small child angel, sent to keep Boy company

GIRL: A baby girl—the twin.

Setting

The interior of the mummy's tummy.

Time

Present day.

ACT ONE

SCENE ONE

The interior of mummy's tummy. There is a small cot, a table, and three chairs. All is dark.

We hear footsteps and a grunt, followed by the sound of a toy being knocked to the floor.

UNCLE RUDOLPHO
Dad-gum it! How come it's so dark in here?

BOY
Who's that?

UNCLE RUDOLPHO
Where's the dratted light?

We hear more clatter and the sound of various things getting bumped into.

UNCLE RUDOLPHO
Ah! Here it is!

A light is switched on, and we see UNCLE RUDOLPHO standing with one knee on a chair, leaning over the table. BOY is sitting up on the small cot, looking at him.

BOY
Who are you?

(UNCLE RUDOLPHO straightens up, brushes himself off, and bows.)

UNCLE RUDOLPHO
I'm your great, great, great, great (is that three or four? . . . oh, whatever)

granduncle Rudolpho, world traveler, travel guide extraordinaire, man about town, the one who KNOWS whatever there is to know.

                    BOY
Oh. Gee. That's a long name.

                 UNCLE RUDOLPHO
You can call me Uncle Bob then.

                    BOY
Uncle Bob? Is that short for Rudolpho?

                 UNCLE RUDOLPHO
No, it's just short.

          (UNCLE RUDOLPHO looks around at the
          clutter of toys and grimaces.)

                 UNCLE RUDOLPHO
What a mess! Didn't they send anybody to clean up? How come the light was off, anyway?

                    BOY
I didn't know I had a light. I didn't know I had anything, until today when I found my other toe.

          (BOY looks down at his feet and
          lifts up one toe.)

                    BOY
This was getting all worn out—I was chewing on it so much.

          (He lifts up his other toe.)

                    BOY
Then I saw this other one. Wow. Was I surprised. It's exactly the same. But fresher.

          (UNCLE RUDOLPHO nods knowingly.)

                 UNCLE RUDOLPHO
Aha! The Other Toe Day. I remember it quite well myself. That must be why my dear wife

Valerina said it was time for me to come
visit.

> (He sighs.)

I just wish she hadn't interrupted my bridge
game. Oh well. I was losing, so, no matter.

> (He claps his hands briskly and eyes
> the room critically.)

                    UNCLE RUDOLPHO
It's time to get things going here!

> (He strides to the wall and vigor-
> ously yanks on a bell pull.)

                    UNCLE RUDOLPHO
Hallo up there! Tummy Angel! Are you there!
We need you down here. The joint's a mess!

                    TUMMY ANGEL
                    (offstage)
Coming! Coming right away!

> (TUMMY ANGEL runs in from stage right,
> looking somewhat flustered. He's carry-
> ing a large cookie in his hand, and is
> chewing and trying to swallow.)

                    TUMMY ANGEL
Are you the Travel Guide?

> (UNCLE RUDOLPHO bows again.)

                    UNCLE RUDOLPHO
That's me! Uncle Rudolpho, at your service.
And you are?

                    TUMMY ANGEL
I'm the new Tummy Angel. Junior grade, I'm
afraid. I'll do my best, but this is my
first case. Do you have any more cookies?

> (TUMMY ANGEL skips over to the cot
> and stares at BOY.)

                    TUMMY ANGEL
Hi! Oh, you're a boy. I thought it was going
to be a girl. Do you have any cookies? I
love cookies. Do you wanna play? We're supposed to play a lot so you can get ready.

          (BOY stands up gingerly and
          stretches. He walks around the room
          and looks at the chairs, and the ta-
          ble, and picks up a toy. He puts the
          toy down and tugs at UNCLE
          RUDOLPHO'S sleeve.)

                    BOY
I feel really confused. What's going on?
What's a cookie?

          (UNCLE RUDOLPHO sits down and pats
          the chair.)

                 UNCLE RUDOLPHO
Come on, boys. Sit down, and let Uncle
Rudolpho tell you all about it.

          (BOY and TUMMY ANGEL sit and look at
          him expectantly.)

                 UNCLE RUDOLPHO
You're a boy. Did you know that? That's why
we call you BOY. At least until later.

                    BOY
No! Really? What's a boy?

          (UNCLE RUDOLPHO sighs.)

                 UNCLE RUDOLPHO
Oh boy, oh boy.

                    BOY
Yes?

                 UNCLE RUDOLPHO
No, not you! Let's start at the beginning.
Do you know where you are?

                    TUMMY ANGEL
North Carolina?

                    UNCLE RUDOLPHO
Tummy Angel! Shush!

          (UNCLE RUDOLPHO leans over and takes
          BOY'S hand.)

                    UNCLE RUDOLPHO
There's a big person, just like me, but
she's prettier . . .

                    (he looks at the audience)
. . . I have to say that you know—and she's
your mummy. You can call her Mummy. And
you'll never guess where you are!

          (BOY rubs his chin and looks around,
          a bit worried.)

                    BOY
North Carolina?

                    UNCLE RUDOLPHO
No, no, no! You're in your mummy's tummy!

                    BOY
What's a tummy?

                    UNCLE RUDOLPHO
Here! Just like mine!

          (UNCLE RUDOLPHO pats his stomach.)

                    BOY
Really! No wonder it was so dark.

                    TUMMY ANGEL
We're not in North Carolina?

          (UNCLE RUDOLPHO glares at TUMMY
          ANGEL.)

                    UNCLE RUDOLPHO
                 (to the audience)
At the moment, I think we're on Route 95.

Suddenly, the three of them tip out
of their chairs.

TUMMY ANGEL

What was that?

(UNCLE RUDOLPHO strides to a wall
and looks through a small telescope
that is planted into the wall. The
large end of the telescope is off
stage.)

UNCLE RUDOLPHO

Well, well, I was wrong. We're not on Route
95 after all. I think that was Mummy and
folks, getting out of their mini-van. They
must be home early.

BOY AND TUMMY ANGEL
(together)

Let me see!

(BOY and TUMMY ANGEL and UNCLE
RUDOLPHO gather around the spyglass,
jostling for space. UNCLE RUDOLPHO
firmly keeps control of the telescope, helping BOY and TUMMY ANGEL
look through it. UNCLE RUDOLPHO then
takes a long look.)

UNCLE RUDOLPHO

Oh no. Don't do that, my good lady.

(UNCLE RUDOLPHO looks at TUMMY ANGEL.)

UNCLE RUDOLPHO

Do you know what she's doing?

TUMMY ANGEL

No, but I like her. She likes cookies, too.
I saw her eat one.

(UNCLE RUDOLPHO, TUMMY ANGEL, and
BOY start to quiver and jerk spasmodically and stumble around the
stage uncontrollably.)

UNCLE RUDOLPHO

Why'd she have to go and do that! I hate it when they do that.

TUMMY ANGEL

What happened?

BOY

I think I'm going to be sick.

UNCLE RUDOLPHO

No! Don't be sick! There's no way to clean it up!

TUMMY ANGEL

What's happening, Mr. Travel Guide?

UNCLE RUDOLPHO

I'm afraid, my dear Tummy Angel, that the boy's mummy has indulged herself in a very large cup of gourmet coffee.

TUMMY ANGEL

Oh, no! If she keeps that up, Boy will become a break dancer when he grows up!

(UNCLE RUDOLPHO and TUMMY ANGEL and BOY settle down on the bed, wiping their brows.)

UNCLE RUDOLPHO

My, oh my. How in the world will Boy get any sleep if his mummy keeps drinking coffee!

TUMMY ANGEL

He'll need a lotta sleep if he becomes a break dancer.

BOY

I'm confused.

UNCLE RUDOLPHO

Don't worry, Boy. We'll explain . . .

(UNCLE RUDOLPHO, TUMMY ANGEL, and BOY suddenly fall off the couch in a heap.)

                    TUMMY ANGEL
Eeeek!!

          (The three of them start to slide
          from left to right, with their arms
          flailing wildly. UNCLE RUDOLPHO strug-
          gles to the telescope and looks out.)

                    BOY
What is it, Uncle Rudolpho?

                    UNCLE RUDOLPHO
That must have been one strong cup of
coffee. Your mummy is doing aerobics! Uh,
oh! Hold on!

          (His glasses askew, UNCLE RUDOLPHO
          clutches his hat as the three of
          them stumble wildly.)

                    UNCLE RUDOLPHO
That was a pushup.

                    BOY
Is it going to be like this from now on?

                    TUMMY ANGEL
It's those modern women, Boy. Your mummy's
a fitness fanatic.

                    UNCLE RUDOLPHO
In my day, women were civilized. Exercise
was strictly forbidden.

                    TUMMY ANGEL
They were too busy with their washboards to
get washboard abs.

                    BOY
What's a washboard?

                    TUMMY ANGEL
We gotta teach you everything, don't we?

                    UNCLE RUDOLPHO
Now, Tummy Angel. Be nice if you want to
get any more cookies!

    (UNCLE RUDOLPHO looks through the
    telescope.)

              UNCLE RUDOLPHO
Ah-ha! Just as I thought!

              TUMMY ANGEL
What is it?

    (UNCLE RUDOLPHO motions them over
    to the telescope, and they look
    through it.)

              UNCLE RUDOLPHO
Modern women are so predictable. After they
exercise, they always take a bath! I can't
imagine why. In my day, we just used perfume.

              BOY
What's that wet stuff?

              TUMMY ANGEL
That's hot water. See the steam? Your
mummy's lying down in the tub. You can tell
because her tummy's too big to fit under the
water. That's why it's getting hot in here.

    (UNCLE RUDOLPHO wipes the sweat off
    his brow.)

              UNCLE RUDOLPHO
Hot is right! We should open a window.

              BOY
Ooooh. What are those other things floating around?

              TUMMY ANGEL
Let me see. Oh, those are sea monsters. If
you're bad, they'll eat you.

    (UNCLE RUDOLPHO grabs the telescope
    and looks through it. He glares at
    TUMMY ANGEL.)

> UNCLE RUDOLPHO

Tummy Angel! What's gotten into you! Those aren't sea monsters! Those are rubber duckies!

> BOY

Will they eat me?

> UNCLE RUDOLPHO

No, no, no. They're toys, to play with. Obviously, your mummy has had a stressful day at the office. By playing with rubber duckies, she can get in touch with her inner child.

> BOY

She's coming for a visit?

> UNCLE RUDOLPHO

No, no, no. She . . .

> > *Just then, they hear a commotion from off stage.*

> (BOY jumps on the bed and pulls the blanket up to his chin.)

> BOY

Is it Mummy?

> (UNCLE RUDOLPHO and TUMMY ANGEL stare at each other.)

> UNCLE RUDOLPHO

I don't think it's medically possible.

> TUMMY ANGEL

It's a sea monster. I just know it.

> (As the three of them stare in consternation, a hand, followed by an arm, enters the room.)

> TUMMY ANGEL

It's an arm.

(. . . and then, with a skip and a
hop, the arm is followed by GIRL. She
stops and looks at them, gravely,
with her thumb in her mouth.)

                    GIRL
Is this Kansas?

                    UNCLE RUDOLPHO
Kansas?

                    TUMMY ANGEL
Kansas?

                    BOY
What's a Kansas?

                    UNCLE RUDOLPHO
Why would you think you were in Kansas,
my dear?

                    GIRL
Well, I was lying in my bed, examining my
other toe that I just found today for the
first time, and then all of a sudden, everything moved around, and I fell off the bed,
and then everything went up and down, and
then it started getting really hot, and
then I thought I had better open a window,
and then I found this door, and here I am.

                    BOY
What did she say?

                    TUMMY ANGEL
She said she's not in Kansas anymore.

          (UNCLE RUDOLPHO nods wisely and
          takes GIRL'S hand. He leads her over
          to the cot where BOY is sitting and
          helps her sit down next to BOY.)

                    UNCLE RUDOLPHO
Boy, you've got good news.

                    BOY
I do?

                    UNCLE RUDOLPHO
Yes, sirree. I'm proud to introduce you to
your twin sister!

                    (to Girl)
Young lady, this is your twin brother! His
name is Boy.

                    TUMMY ANGEL
Well, I never. Do you have any cookies?

                    GIRL
I don't think so.

                    (to Uncle Rudolpho)
Do I have any cookies?

                    UNCLE RUDOLPHO
Not yet, my sweet. But you will.

            (UNCLE RUDOLPHO stands and takes
            TUMMY ANGEL'S hand.)

                    UNCLE RUDOLPHO
Well, Tummy Angel. It's time for us to
leave. We've done our duty and helped guide
these delightful young people through the
excitement of The Other Toe Day. They'll be
fine now.

                    TUMMY ANGEL
When we get back upstairs, can I have a cookie?

                    UNCLE RUDOLPHO
You can have two. One for each of them.

                    TUMMY ANGEL
Goodie!!!

            (UNCLE RUDOLPHO kisses BOY and GIRL
            on the cheek.)

                    UNCLE RUDOLPHO
Well, good-bye then. Take care of each other.
You must have a lot to talk about now.

                    BOY AND GIRL
Yes sir!

                        BOY
                    (to Girl)
So you have another toe, too?

                        GIRL
I sure do. You wanna see it? It's really
clean and tastes pretty good.

                    (BOY and GIRL bend over, staring at
                    their toes. They don't notice as the
                    light goes dim, and UNCLE RUDOLPHO
                    and TUMMY ANGEL exit.)

                    TUMMY ANGEL
                        (o.s.)
Mr. Travel Guide, are you sure they'll be ok?

                    UNCLE RUDOLPHO
                        (o.s.)
Most certainly! That is, until they discover
they have eight little toes too. We wouldn't
want them to over-nibble, you know.

                    TUMMY ANGEL
                        (o.s.)
No, that would be bad, wouldn't it? Can I
have a cookie now?

                    UNCLE RUDOLPHO
                        (o.s.)
Tummy Angel! Whatever shall I do with you?

                    As the light goes dark, we
                    hear peals of laughter
                    from Uncle Rudolpho and
                    Tummy Angel.

                        CURTAIN.

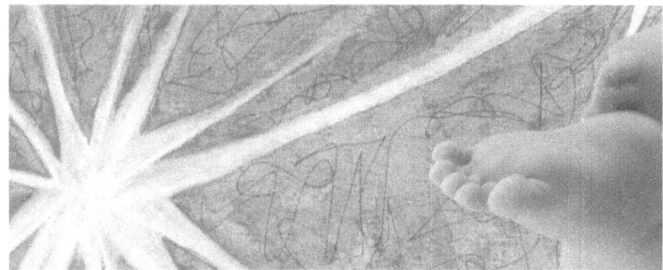

Bogey the Magnificent

A story for every child who has ever lost a dog

*L*et me tell you about the special day that Bogey got a new coat. First, I have to tell you about Bogey the Magnificent. If you were one of those wonderful people whom Bogey consented to love and had arrived at his door with the thought of Doggie Cookies in your head, he would have wagged his tail and wiggled his body and kissed your face until you had fallen over in a heap on the floor and hollered, "Enough!" You would have known who Bogey was then.

Bogey was a Wiggle Dog. No one up the street, or down the street, or even around the block, could wiggle more than he. Perhaps it was because he was part Norwich Terrier (or so he proudly told the other dogs). It might have been because he had a long, furry, orange coat that gleamed in the sunlight. Or because of his pointed kitty-cat ears. Vinny the Gangster Cat, who made it his business to roughhouse with Bogey, always told Bogey that any dog with kitty-cat ears was okay in his book.

After Bogey had wiggled for a while, he would practice barking. He had an out-of-the-ordinary bark, in a special code, known only to those "in the know." It was a secret, five-bark, "Woo, woo, woo, woo, woo!" that very clearly was impatiently directed at his Master and Mistress and their Four Lovely Children. He used his imperious bark when he wanted to come into the house and had had enough of waiting for those Lazy Humans to get him.

Did they not know that his name was short for Humphrey Bogart the Movie Star? Did they not realize that he was also known throughout the land as the Great and Majestic "Orange Julius," a direct descendent of Julius Caesar the Eighth, who wagged his tail at the soda pop stand on the corner of 8th and Main? If this were not true, then why did his Mistress call him Orange Julius? Since Bogey was very wiggly and was often busily barking, he never, ever heard the birds in the trees when they called down to him with kind, little chirps and said, "Dear Doggie, it's because your coat is orange."

Whenever Vinny the Gangster Cat heard His Majesty bark, he just sputtered and harrumphed, and slyly hissed, "Humphrey Bogart had bad teeth, you know." The squirrels thought that was very funny and would scamper up and down the tree limbs, just out of reach, and squeak, "Bad teeth! Bad teeth!"

Orange Julius Bogey the Magnificent ignored them all, for he knew a great secret. His specialized five-bark code always worked! So, with enough wiggles to mix up a fruit smoothie, he would greet his Master or Mistress or one of their Lovely Children when they very obediently came outside to get him, and he would say, with just a hint of condescension, "Did you really have to take so long?"

He never waited long enough for an explanation. Why should one wait for trifles, when Vinny the Gangster Cat was just inside the door, already in his running shoes, getting ready for a race? If that wasn't enough to distract a Royal Wiggle Dog, there was the Large Yellow Labrador who was always willing to play the Bite Game.

Have you never heard of the Bite Game? It's really a lot of fun, you know. You take your mouth and open wide, baring all of your teeth, and then you firmly press down on the biggest bite of fur that you can grab, and then you pull and pull, and growl and growl. Then you run as fast as ever you can because the Large Yellow Labrador is actually much better at playing Bite than middle-sized Norwich Terriers, even ones of Royal blood.

At first, Bogey the Magnificent didn't like the Large Yellow Labrador. She was named "Indi." What kind of name was that anyway? She just showed up in the kitchen one day, small and squirmy, and smelling like wet puppies. She didn't even know how to poo. It was with many sighs of Kingly tolerance that Bogey slowly managed to teach the little squirt what was up. He practiced growling at her loudly, just to show her who was really the Boss. When she trembled and cowered at his magnificence, he grandly waved his paw and said, "You may stay, my child."

Then she grew. And grew and grew and grew, until Bogey could have driven his sports car right under her tummy! She was that big! It was exceedingly unfair, and Bogey spent many a night browsing the Internet looking for the phone number of the Dogs' Union for Unfair Growth Practices until one of the Lovely Children caught him in the act and said, "Bogey! Dogs can't go on the Internet! And how did you get the password anyway?"

Grumbling, Sir Bogey decided that he must put up with Her Largeness. Luckily for him, Indi was a kind, sweet young thing. She would often press her cheek against his and say, in her soft Southern accent, "You're the One, Bogey!"

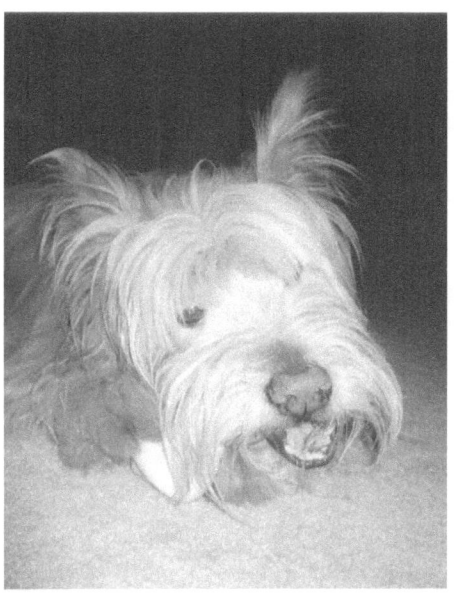

After playing the Bite Game in front of the television during movie night, which was always a thrill because it made the Master mad since he couldn't see the TV, Bogey and Indi would spend a great deal of time staring at the dinner plates. You may wonder why dogs would stare at dinner plates, but if you had seen the pizza crusts just sitting there, what would you have done?

The Mistress was very kind, which is as it should be. She could always be counted on to throw Bogey a "Pizza Bone," as she so quaintly called the bits of crust. He didn't mind what she called them as long as she obeyed his "Loud and Persistent Pizza-Bone Whine," which was a great specialty of his. Indi and Vinny were quite jealous of his talented whining and often asked him where he got his Degree.

Bogey couldn't remember, but since he was a kind Leader, he did warn them that Pizza Bone Chewing was almost as bad as cigarette smoking. He would open his mouth and mutter, "See my teeth? Do as I say, not as I do!"

It was a sad fact that after many years of Pizza Bone Chewing, Bogey's lower front teeth were in a terrible state of disrepair. He was nine years old and was feeling creaky and rickety. He felt inclined to sleep a lot, between playing the Bite Game and chasing Vinny the Gangster Cat. His long, furry, orange coat was getting white and a bit straggly. He asked Indi if she knew which shampoo would fix his split ends, but she was no help at all. She just smiled and murmured, "My Kingy Thingy, you're getting old. But I love you."

He still had juice, though. He was, after all, Bogey the Magnificent Orange Julius. On the cloudy morning of August the 12th, 2008, which on the Dog Calendar is known as "The Day to Get Rabbits before the Snow Comes in Maine," he decided that it was every King's right to travel and see the sights.

Being a resourceful Wiggle Dog, he pulled back and forth until the old spring on his very personal leash went "Pop!" and he was off! He ran this way and that way, and up the yard and down the yard. Freedom was a glorious thing, and Bogey the Magnificent was Proud and Happy to be On the Run.

It might have been a cat or a squirrel or even a low-flying birdie that caught his eye. He hasn't told anyone yet, but perhaps one day he will. Whatever it was, the thrill of the chase coursed through his getting-old veins with a glorious command to run, Bogey, run!

He ran and ran and forgot all about the rule that even Kingly Dogs should look both ways before crossing the street. A vehicle roaring down Main Street interrupted his Adventure, much to his annoyance. He was very perplexed as he saw the truck speeding away, leaving his body on the road. He sniffed it and thought it very odd that it looked like a carbon copy of himself.

A nice lady came along and took his body to the vet's, down the street. It was just two blocks away from his home, so Bogey decided not to follow her. Why should he? She was carrying something that looked like him, but she obviously didn't see that he was sitting right there on the grass by the road! He barked at her, but she couldn't hear him, so he turned around and went back to his yard and lay down under his favorite tree, and forgot all about the lady.

After a while, his Mistress came out, then his Master, and then the Lovely Girl Child. They looked right at him, but couldn't even see him! He did his five-bark code many times, but they didn't even hear one of his barks. They called him and called him, so he went right up to them and smiled at them and wagged his Kingly tail, but for some strange reason, they couldn't see him. He wondered if they had lost their minds. He had heard about such things.

He watched them all day, as they drove around town and walked through the woods, calling his name. He watched as they went to the vet and came back crying, around dinnertime. Since he loved them, he tried kissing them with his special Wiggly Kisses, but they didn't rub his back or anything. Later that night, after they had gone to bed, he sat in the kitchen and talked with Vinny the Gangster Cat. At least Vinny could see him!

Vinny rubbed against him, and looked him up and down and said,

"Hey, Wiggle Dog! What's with the shiny new coat? Did you use a new shampoo? Where'd you buy it? Can I use it?"

Bogey was surprised, and said, "New coat? What do you mean, Gangster Boy?"

"Your coat, stupid! It's shiny and fluffy, the way every cat's coat should be. And your teeth! Zowie, wowie, man! You got new teeth! Not bad! What's your scam?"

Bogey was quite astonished at this new turn of events. He climbed up on top of the kitchen table, which was, of course, entirely Off Limits, and stood over the round hair-cutting mirror that was lying on the table. The Gangster Cat was right! His missing lower teeth were back, and his coat was a thing of pride! He looked at Vinny and said, "What do you expect? I'm a King!"

The next morning, he greeted everyone with a Wiggle and a Bark but again got no response. He went up into the field that morning with his Mistress and his Lovely Girl Child and watched them as they dug a hole. He loved digging holes, so he tried to help them, but for some reason, his paws couldn't quite catch the dirt.

Around 2 p.m., as he was sunning himself under his favorite tree, he was surprised to see his Master carrying something that looked just like him. The Master put it down next to him, and then the Mistress and the Lovely Girl Child came out of the house, with Indi in tow.

He was happy to see her, and said, "Hey Girl! What's going on?"

Indi smiled at him and then went up to his body that lay on the sheet and sniffed it. The Master and Mistress bent down and patted Indi, and said, "Bogey's gone away, Indi."

Indi looked at them and looked at his body on the sheet, and then looked at Bogey, and said, "You're going away, Bogey darling?"

He didn't think he was going away, but things were feeling kind of strange. He jumped up and barked at his Master and Mistress and said, "Hey, Guys! I'm standing right here! Look at my new coat! You didn't even have to give me a bath! Look how shiny it is!"

They didn't see him, though. They carried his body up to the top of the hill by a big tree, and put it in the hole that they had dug, and put flowers on his body. His Mistress read some beautiful words from a paper that she had written on, and they touched his body and prayed and said they loved him. He liked that and barked in agreement. They said that they would see him someday, and he liked that too. They covered his body with dirt and sod and put flowers and a stone on the top.

Then they said, "Good-bye, Bogey!" and hugged and went back down the hill to the house.

Bogey sat at the top of the hill and watched them as they went into the house. Indi saw him through the door and smiled and barked.

He didn't know quite what to do. He thought about staying in the house with them, even though they couldn't see him. As he was sitting by his grave, he heard a sound behind him. Looking around, he saw his old friends, Rupert the Placid Cat and Hobbes the Gangly Jumping Dog. They had left for parts unknown some time ago, when they all lived in Virginia, where there were no squirrels in the yard (much to Bogey's disgust). What was more exciting than barking at squirrels?

Rupert and Hobbes came over and sniffed him, and said, "Nice coat, Bogey!" and "Wow! Shiny Coat!"

They talked about old times, sat in the sun, and looked down the hill at the house. Rupert, who always knew things before anyone else, explained all about the new home that Bogey was going to live in. Bogey was quite pleased to hear that there were thousands of squirrels who absolutely loved to play tag with Kingly Dogs with Orange Coats.

He was thrilled indeed to hear that one day his Master and Mistress and Lovely Girl Child and the Three Handsome Boy Guys would all live there too, and would give him Pizza Bones to chew on every single night! Vinny the Gangster Cat and Indi the Southern Belle would also come, along with Minnie the Squeaky Fragile Cat, and lots of other animal friends. Nothing would ever prevent Bogey Orange Julius from Wiggling and Barking and doing what he did best, which was, of course, to live like a King.

After a while, Rupert and Hobbes stretched, and got up and started walking toward the woods. Bogey followed them, but as he reached the edge of the woods, he turned and looked at the house and barked. It was his very best and most special bark and carried with it across the field to the house all the codes and words he had learned in his nine years of Wiggly life. He barked again, five times in all—his lovely-to-hear "woo, woo, woo, woo, woo" bark that this time meant, "I'll see you soon."

Rupert and Hobbes smiled at him, and then the three of them walked into the woods and were gone. No, not gone. Not that kind of gone.

On a sunny day, they might visit again and ask for Pizza Bones and Kitty Cat Treats. It's what they do.

This story was written for our youngest child, Tadin,
who was away from home when our dog Bogey was hit by a car.

The Christmas Mission of
King Hedley the Hedgehog

I've often been told that on the day I was born, enough rain fell in our county to fill two ponds and a dozen bathtubs. It sounded like an exaggeration to me, but I was small, so what did I know? It certainly was true that on the night before my birth, there was so much wind and rain that Papa couldn't come home to our palace, and so had stayed in a neighbor's nest. It was a long night for Mama, but when I was born, right after breakfast, she sang a lovely song in a tired, contented little voice. Two of our most faithful hedgehog servants ignored the storm and ran through the rain and across the fields to tell my father the momentous news of my birth.

King Roly-Poly, or Papa, as our family called him, was very happy to hear the news. He loved me very much and would spend hours bouncing me on his tummy, winking at my Mama, Queen Gertrude the Firm-Nosed. Mama was a practical soul but smiled anyway.

I was happy for a while, but then things began to Happen. Papa choked on a bit of root and went to a better place. Mama was very distressed but insisted that I be immediately crowned King of all the English Hedgehogs.

A large group of Hedgehog Ministers traveled up from London and witnessed my coronation. Thus, at a very young age, I became King Hedley, the Defender of All Hedgehogs Everywhere—even Scotland.

I heard that the Scottish hedgehogs didn't approve of me, contesting that my Papa was an Interloper and could not possibly be the True King. My sister Margaret Moopie winked at me across the dinner table one night and said that the real reason the Scots didn't like Papa was that he hated haggis. I didn't like haggis either, so to this day, the Scots insist upon calling me "Hedley the Anti-Haggis." Sigh. The trials of Kingship are many.

I enjoyed being King but soon realized that very few Humans understood the rightful place of Hedgehogs in the Grand Scheme of the Universe. Knocking over one's home is really the height of rudeness, and English farmers should know better. When Farmer Francis Snowden-Micklethwaite cut the hedges down over our palace one day, we knew that it was time to move.

So, on a rainy spring morning, Mama and my sisters and brothers got in their carriage and rode southwest toward Wales and more hospitable climes. Since I was the King, I took it upon myself to travel to London to consult with the High Council of Hedgehog Ministers about our plans for a Hedgehog Bill of Rights.

I must say that London is a nasty place for hedgehogs. There I was, peacefully trotting across Piccadilly Square, when a lorry came zooming up the road and almost flattened me! It was not the right way to treat a King.

I had no way of knowing that the worst was yet to come. Being tired from my long journey, I snuggled up on top of some nice wooden boxes. I slept very well and dreamed of wood chips and turnips.

You can imagine my shock when I awoke and realized that the nice wooden boxes were no longer sitting on the sidewalk outside the London Harbor Master's warehouse. No indeed. They were securely lashed inside a big metal box that was darker than the underside of an old tree. Everything was rocking back and forth, and I heard cries of "Whoa! Did you see that whale?" outside the metal box.

Well, I'm sure you can guess what took me the whole journey to figure out. I had ended up on a freighter to America! Did I mention that things had begun to happen? Sigh. The trials of Kingship are many.

When the ship arrived in New York, the big metal box was swung onto a dock and put on a truck and driven to a warehouse and opened with a clang and a screech and a banging of  doors. I snuck out, as any good hedgehog knows how to do, and strolled in a very dignified fashion, far from that dreadful place. Well, I scampered actually, but please don't alert the media.

Have you been to New York? It's even worse than London! It was interesting, however, that I heard many of the humans saying, "Oy!" That word is often used in London, although I think it means something different there.

I won't tell you of all my adventures in the Big Apple. Suffice it to say that one day I was sunbathing in Central Park, yawning and stretching, when a birdie hopped right onto my tummy. It was an extraordinary bird. Its feathers were a golden colour, and it said its name was Hoopoozoopoowoopoo. It was one of those American Indian Spirit Birds, I think. We don't have such birds in England, more's the pity.

 Anyway, "Hoop" proceeded to tell me that I had been brought to America for a Reason. It seems that I had a Mission (as well I should, for I am a King, you know). Hoop talked a long time about Kings and Cats and Lewis Carroll, and then he mentioned Utah.

"Utah?" I asked.

Hoop looked at me with exasperation. "You haven't been listening at all!" he scolded. "Yes, Utah! That's where Alicia lives!"

"Who's Alicia?" I asked. Oh my. What a screeching and scolding I got from Hoopoozoopoowoopoo after that! It seemed that Princess Alicia was a Very Important Person who lived near Salt Lake City. I gathered that she was more important than the Governor or the Mayor. And need I mention that Hoop said she was lovely and charming? And sweet. And nice. And smart. She even kept her room clean, by all accounts.

After quite a long speech, Hoop stared at me and said, "You have to go there and live with Princess Alicia and be her friend. We have decided that she needs a Hedgehog who is a King (not just a common, hardworking hedgehog, but a King) to keep her company. Every girl needs a fuzzy, fluffy, handsome Hedgehog Friend who can roll up into a little ball and smile."

Hoop fluttered his wings and declared, "King Hedley, you have been Chosen."

Well, I have to tell you that when an American Indian Spirit Bird named Hoopoozoopoowoopoo gives you an order, you don't question it, even if you are a King.

Thus, I shook his wing and thanked him, and immediately set out for Utah. I had no idea where Utah was, but someone said it was west of New York.

They forgot to tell me that it was four billion hedgehog miles away, but we English keep a stiff upper lip and never complain. Even during the Battle of Britain, we just said it was "a bit noisy outside." So, I won't go on and on about the strange trucks that I rode in, or the motorcycle gangs that I hitched a ride with, or the night I spent in a police station, or the bumper sticker that said, "Who Will Hug the Porcupine?" That one gave me a shiver. Have you ever tried to hug a porcupine? My cousin Germaine tried, and she was very sorry afterwards.

I started out from New York in early summer, and would you believe that it took me until December to arrive in Utah? That's almost as slow as taking a wagon train!

I have to say that the moment I arrived at Princess Alicia's house was the grandest and most exciting event of my life. It was better than being crowned King. It was better than turnips and cheese or marmalade on toast. I met the young lady's parents first. They were extremely polite and had roots in the old country. I must visit Denmark one day and go skiing, followed by a trip to the Vatican to meet the Pope.

Alicia's Papa and Mama told me to hide under the Christmas Tree, which I thought was very intelligent. I snuggled up against the base of the tree and dreamed of Prince Albert and Queen Victoria, who also liked Christmas trees very much.

I spent the night snoozing under the tree and was briefly awakened by an overly large gentleman in a red coat, who came in very quietly and winked at me before he put some packages under the tree. I was going to wink back, but he was gone before I could properly position my eyelid. He seemed to be in an awful hurry.

Finally, the morning came! After traveling over two thousand miles from New York, and all that way from my palace under the hedgerow in Merry Old England, the moment arrived when Princess Alicia stood in front of that lovely Christmas Tree. I was very excited as she opened her presents, wondering if she would see my quivering little nose in between the boxes of gifts.

And then she found me! It was magnificent, you know, meeting Princess Alicia. With the most courteous bow that a hedgehog could possibly muster, I graciously presented myself to her. I, His Majesty, King Hedley, the King of All Hedgehogs in England, the One who does not eat haggis, and the one who was given the very, very honorable and special and lovely Mission to be Alicia's friend! I wished her a Happy Christmas and immediately fell asleep.

I was tired!

This story was written for a very real Alicia who lived in Utah, and, on one fine Christmas morning, received a fluffy and very Kingly hedgehog, sitting quite grandly in a box.

About the Author

It's common for "About the Author" sections to be short bits of prose written in the third person. I've never seen one that included photos, as this one does. I've decided to break the rules and not only include photos but also write this section in the first person, and write more than a little snippet.

Although David Copperfield began his story with the chapter heading "I Am Born," I shall refrain from telling you that I was born under a canoe on Miami Beach while the moon gazed sympathetically at my mother as she was pelted with coconuts by monkeys howling in the palm trees.

I cannot say that my birth happened that way, for it did not, since I was instead born in a hospital in Coral Gables, Florida, in 1954, two months premature. It was quite unexciting but not dull, at least from my mother's point of view.

My mother, Polly Kapteyn Brown, was my best friend throughout my childhood. Although she was not a "huggy" type of person, she was someone whom I could trust and love and respect.

I arrived in life in the footsteps of my ancestors, starting with my parents. I owe them a profound debt for the goodness and merit that they left behind. In particular, my mother believed in my potential and gave me the vision, while I was young, to try to think on a grand philosophical scale. (I am still attempting to do that.) Polly was an artist and art teacher, first at the Portland School of Fine and Applied Arts (the precursor to MECA, the Maine College of Art), and then at a school called "Concept" that she founded with some fellow artists, including the noted Maine artist Bill Manning. In 1982, a year before she died from lung cancer, she earned a graduate degree from the Episcopal Divinity School in Cambridge, Massachusetts.

She was also a writer, poet, and philosopher, perhaps inspired by her aunt, and my grandaunt, Olga Fröbe-Kapteyn, a Dutch spiritualist, theosophist, and scholar. Olga was the founder of the Eranos Foundation in Ascona, Switzerland, and was a friend of Carl Gustav Jung's.

Olga was, in turn, inspired by her mother and my great-grandmother, Geertruida Agneta Kapteyn-Muysken, a humanist and leading social activist in nineteenth-century London. She was influenced by the French poet and philosopher Jean-Marie Guyau and counted George Bernard Shaw and Prince Pyotr Alexeyevich Kropotkin among her large circle of friends. She was an influential writer in London for twenty years and then moved to Zurich, where she became the center of a group of artists and  students. Many Polish and Russian student émigrés regarded her as their "spiritual mother."[1]

This lineage of writers was unknown to me when I was a student. I believed that it was from my mother alone that I had inherited my passion for writing. I was thus quite fascinated when I learned more about the lives of Olga and Geertruida.

---

1. MUYSKEN, Geertruida Agneta. BWSA - Biografisch Woordenboek van het. Socialisme en de Arbeidersbeweging in Nederland. https://socialhistory.org/bwsa/biografie/muysken Web page viewed on December 10, 2016

My confidence to follow a writing career was also bolstered in my high school days, when my senior-class English teacher at the Waynflete School in Portland, the late William Ackley, said to me, "Brownie, you've got it. Keep going!" (Or something to that effect.) I kept going and am immensely grateful for his encouragement.

I am indeed fortunate to have met and married a wonderful lady who is also a writer and spiritualist, my dear bride, Kimmy Sophia. I affectionately call her "the Forest Queen." For many years, we co-published *The Significato Journal,* an online magazine with the theme "nectar for the soul" that emphasized the arts, nature, spirituality, and service. That magazine closed in 2020. The content has been moved to our respective websites (peterfalkenberg-brown.com and kimmysophiabrown.com). We reside in my home state of Maine and have four grown children.

My father, Carl Falkenberg Brown, was the son of Norman Brown of Portland, Maine, and the Baroness Helen Dean Falkenberg, of Quebec City. "Granny" and her four siblings each inherited their titles from their father, Baron Fredrick Andreas Falkenberg, since their family received the title in 1733, starting with my fifth great-grandfather Gabriel Henriksson Falkenberg of

Trystorp, Sweden, and thus by Swedish law did not follow the tradition of primogeniture.

Baron Gabriel married Countess Beata Margareta Douglas and was the grandson of Cunradt von Falkenberg, born in 1591.

My second great-grandfather Baron Gerhard Knut Alfrid Falkenberg was appointed Consul General to British North America in the 1800s and thus moved to Quebec, where eventually, my grandfather Norman met Baroness Helen and brought her back to Portland, Maine.

Falkenberg
af Trystorp
Friherrliga ätten nr 255

Since I have a great love of history and grew up looking at the coat of arms of the Falkenbergs of Trystorp, I contacted cousins who shared the history of my paternal grandmother's side of the family.

On the Brown side, Carl was the great-grandson of William Wentworth Brown, who purchased and developed what was to become the Brown Company in Berlin, New Hampshire. Second great-grandfather William (known as "W.W.") was the son of a farmer, Jonathan, born in 1776 in Hallowell, Maine.

Jonathan was a devout Christian and held Bible studies in the family home in Clinton, Maine, for forty years. Jonathan's lineage started in America with the arrival in Boston of my seventh great-grandfather William Browne, where he married my seventh great-grandmother Elizabeth Ruggles in 1655.

It is possible that William came from Dunfermline, Scotland, and may have emigrated to America to avoid Oliver Cromwell's armies, which would be ironic, considering that my seventh great-granduncle on my grandmother's side was the ruthless and infamous Charles Fleetwood, commander in chief of Cromwell's armies.

William Wentworth Brown built a logging and paper company that thrived for almost seventy years until the Great Depression and off-shore competition ended its run. At its height, the Brown Company owned four million acres of timberland and had turned tiny Berlin into a thriving town.

W.W. and his sons built a company known for its honesty and its kindness to its employees and the residents of Berlin. Although the family was unable to surmount the challenges of the Depression, a family historian wrote that when they failed, they "failed honorably."

By the time I was born, the Brown money was long gone, leaving my father to struggle and scrape and do his best to raise three children. Since we were poor, our family often returned to live in Granny's house, a large brick manse at 135 Vaughan Street in Portland's prosperous West End. Of all the many places I lived as a child, my grandmother's house was the one that I counted as home.

I've often reflected that growing up "poor" might have been for the best, since who knows what kind of person I would have been if I had been raised in wealth? Life is full of mysteries like that, but I am grateful that many of the wealthy Browns believed in kindness and honesty and

honor. To my mother, most especially, I am thankful that I inherited a deep love for writing and art and nature and music and all things of beauty. I've discovered that being surrounded by those gifts throughout my life gave me the experiential knowledge that I was the very opposite of poor.

I inherited an adventurous spirit from my ancestors. When I was eighteen, in 1973, I rode off into the sunset on a bicycle, headed for Mardi Gras in New Orleans, and then on to California. I spent two weeks traveling through the back roads of New England until I arrived at the Connecticut-New York border. Much to my surprise, after visiting my paternal aunt in New York City, I decided to stay and live in Manhattan.

My bicycle trip had been contemplative and had heightened my sense that I was on a spiritual search. I had kept a picture of Jesus next to my bed since I was four years old and had been inspired by books like *The Robe* by Lloyd C. Douglas, about a Roman soldier who gambled for Jesus' robe, converted to Christianity, and then died a martyr under Roman arrows. I had a strong desire to follow Jesus and wished that I could have been alive when he preached in Israel. My mother had also introduced me to other religious avenues, and as I arrived in New York in my quest to "go west, young man," I was busily reading books by Erich Fromm, J. Krishnamurti, and various Sufi authors.

I stayed in New York for a couple of years and then began a long process of exploring the rest of the country. Along the way, I became a writer, a web database programmer, and the Director of Web Operations for a magazine publishing company in New York City. After thirty-four years of gallivanting, I arrived back in Maine in 2007 with a wife, four children, two dogs, and a cat. A lot happens when you ride away into the sunset.

For many years now, I've been exploring a path that has a great similarity to the one followed by my philosopher mother. I've read many of the same ancient Christian mystics that she studied in her religious quest as an Episcopalian. As I delved into the writings of a broad range of mystics, I discovered what was to become one of my core beliefs—that no one can be closer to a person than the indwelling God. I can say with immense gratitude that I am passionately in love with God.

Partly through my own experience with God, I have developed a profound appreciation for the kind, gentle, compassionate, egalitarian, and respectful love that I feel that God has for each individual.

God is my Great Solace and my Best Friend. Deepening my awareness of God's presence and expressing God's love to others are the central goals of my life, both here and in my future life in the spirit world. I am grateful that my faith in God and my vision about a world of love have been profoundly informed by the mystics who taught about the indwelling God.

My life now is a tremendously exciting adventure—the mystical search to become resonant with the indwelling God of love and kindness and compassion.

It is a search imbued with daily enthusiasm and joy and the conviction that, as Deepak Chopra wrote in *How to Know God: The Soul's Journey into the Mystery of Mysteries*:

God enfolds the whole creation, not just the nice parts.

∽

At Two Lights, Cape Elizabeth, Maine

Image Credits

Color images used inside the book have been converted to grayscale and some images (including the cover) have been cropped or modified.

Cover Image

"Abstract sky painting," by Will
Painting has been cropped, and color has been modified.
Licensed from stock.adobe.com

Cover design by Great Northern Tea

Story Images

Frame designs by Great Northern Tea use images from stock.adobe.com.

Waking Up Dead and Confused Is a Terrible Thing

Drawing of Lucy and Hiram by Great Northern Tea

Drawing of rat:
Togo picture gallery maintained by Database Center for Life Science (DBCLS).
August 15, 2013, (CC BY 3.0)
https://commons.wikimedia.org/wiki/File:Rat_togopic.png
https://creativecommons.org/licenses/by/3.0/deed.en

Vagabond Sleep

Title illustration by Great Northern Tea

The Ad Hoc Committee to Save the Queen

Painting: "Mlle Camargo Dancing"
by Nicolas Lancret. Oil on canvas. 44x55 cm
France. First half of the 18th century. Inv. no. GE-1145
The State Hermitage Museum, St. Petersburg, Russia
http://www.hermitagemuseum.org
Photograph © The State Hermitage Museum. Photo by Vladimir Terebenin.
Used with permission. Painting has been cropped.

Frame design by Great Northern Tea

About Mlle Camargo, from the museum's description:

"Such is this small portrait of one of the most educated women of the 18th
century, friend of the philosophers Helvetius and Voltaire - Marie-Anne Cupis
de Camargo (1710-1770), a famous dancer who introduced numerous
innovations to the ballet, including the ballet pumps used to this day, and new
steps, the pirouette and the fouette."

The Day I Said No to Kim Jong Un

Caricature of Kim Jong Un
by J. Conescu, 2017, (CC BY 2.0), Wikimedia Commons
https://commons.wikimedia.org/wiki/File:
Kim_Jong_Un_-_Caricature_(38063431802).png
https://creativecommons.org/licenses/by/2.0/deed.en

Frame design by Great Northern Tea

The Epiphany of Zebediah Clump

Frame design and collage by Great Northern Tea

Image of Conceptual Venus Transit:
NASA/Goddard Space Flight Center Conceptual Image Lab,
Animator: Walt Feimer

Newspaper image by Peter Falkenberg Brown

Photograph of squirrel from the short film,
"The Epiphany of Zebediah Clump"

Image of Atomic Bomb from footage:
Atom Bomb [Joe Bonica's Movie of the Month] (ca. 1955)
Prelinger Archives, Creative Commons Public Domain License

Photograph of bluejay from the short film,
"The Epiphany of Zebediah Clump"

The Day the Moon Smiled

Image of hand with quill pen with moon in background:
A photograph of the moon was placed by the author in a cropped and edited section of the painting:

"Portrait of Doctor Alphonse Leroy"
by Jacques-Louis David, 1783, Oil on canvas, Height: 72 cm (28.3 in)
One of his pupils, Jean-François Garneray, assisted in painting the hands and fabrics. Collection: Musée Fabre, Public Domain

Frame: cropped section of photo:
VdB4 nebula with NGC225 star cluster, by Jschulman555
December 8, 2012, (CC BY-SA 3.0)
https://commons.wikimedia.org/wiki/File:VdB4_and_NGC225.jpg
https://creativecommons.org/licenses/by-sa/3.0/deed.en

Photo of super moon, 2011
by Dmitry Benbau, Ekaterinburg, Russia. Used with permission

Photo of the far side of the moon by NASA
"This image shows the far side of the moon, illuminated by the sun, as it crosses between the DSCOVR spacecraft's Earth Polychromatic Imaging Camera (EPIC) camera and telescope, and the Earth - one million miles away."
Credits: NASA/NOAA
https://www.nasa.gov/feature/goddard/
from-a-million-miles-away-nasa-camera-shows-moon-crossing-face-of-earth
August 5, 2015

The Captive

Drawing and frame design by Great Northern Tea

The Last Person

Drawing and frame design by Great Northern Tea

Photo of Las Vegas:
Dietmar Rabich / Wikimedia Commons /
"Las Vegas (Nevada, USA), The Strip -- 2012 -- 6232" / CC BY-SA 4.0
https://commons.wikimedia.org/wiki/
File:Las_Vegas_(Nevada,_USA),_The_Strip_--_2012_--_6232.jpg
https://creativecommons.org/licenses/by-sa/4.0/deed

The Orchid Queen

Painting: "Cattleya Orchid and Three Brazilian Hummingbirds"
by Martin Johnson Heade, 1871, oil on panel
Height: 34.8 cm (13.7 in); Width: 45.6 cm (17.9 in)
Collection: National Gallery of Art, Washington, DC, USA, Public Domain

Frame design by Great Northern Tea

Birth

Drawing and design by Great Northern Tea

Chart of human evolution excerpted from "Extinct Humans,"
by Ian Tattersall and Jeffrey H. Schwartz (Westview Press).
Used with permission of Dr. Tattersall. Chart has been cropped.
http://www.amnh.org/our-research/staff-directory/ian-tattersall

The Attack of the Devil Bug Gang

Drawing by Great Northern Tea

The Angel Who Fed the Cat

Drawing by Great Northern Tea
Image of axe from:
Dictionnaire raisonné du mobilier français de l'époque carlovingienne
à la Renaissance - illustration Tome 6
by Viollet-le-Duc, 1874, Public Domain
https://commons.wikimedia.org/wiki/File:06-018.png

Photo of our cat Rupert by family member

The Child in the Forest

Painting: "Rotwild im Waldinneren," ("Red deer in the interior of the forest")
by August Friedrich Kessler, 1852, oil on canvass, 91 x 123 cm
Public Domain. Painting has been cropped.
Frame design by Great Northern Tea

The Journey of Anhad

Drawing and frame design by Great Northern Tea
"Blackout cake, sometimes called Brooklyn Blackout cake"
by Carl Black from Decatur, GA, US, January 4, 2014, (CC BY-SA 2.0)
https://commons.wikimedia.org/wiki/File:Blackout_cake.jpg
https://creativecommons.org/licenses/by-sa/2.0/deed.en

Mock Bug's Escape: The Incident of the Alien Child

Drawing and bottom frame design by Great Northern Tea

Photo of UFO by George Stock (cropped)
"Amateur photographs of alleged UFOs"
New Jersey, July 31, 1952
https://www.cia.gov/library/center-for-the-study-of-intelligence/
csi-publications/csi-studies/studies/97unclass/p69.gif/image.gif
Public Domain

The Sad Tale of Rupert and Eggbert

Painting: "Mäuse," ("Mice") (cropped and flipped with halo added)
by Karl Reichert, before 1918
Watercolor, white gouache, and crayon on paper, 22.5 x 20 cm
Public Domain

Frame design and halo by Great Northern Tea

The Bird That Was Saved by a THING

Drawing and frame design by Great Northern Tea

Photo of sparrow (modified)
"A male House Sparrow in flight"
by "davidgsteadman," June 12, 2010, (CC BY 2.0)
https://commons.wikimedia.org/wiki/File:Sparrow_in_flight.jpg
https://creativecommons.org/licenses/by/2.0/deed.en

The Other Toe Day

Photo of toes by "arizanko"
Licensed from stock.adobe.com
Photo has been modified, with added starbursts

Frame and toe design by Great Northern Tea

Bogey the Magnificent

Photos of Bogey by the Brown family
Frame design by Great Northern Tea

The Christmas Mission of King Hedley the Hedgehog

All sketches by Kimmy Sophia Brown
Frame design by Great Northern Tea

About the Author

Photo of author speaking, from video shot by author

Photo of Polly Kapteyn Brown, photographer unknown

Photo of Olga Fröbe-Kapteyn at Eranos in the 1940s.
Photograph by Margarethe Fellerer, Eranos Foundation Archives
Used with permission of the Fondazione Eranos, Ascona, Switzerland

Photo of Geertruida Agneta Kapteyn-Muysken
Public Domain. G.A. Muysken, Internationaal Archief
voor de Vrouwenbeweging (Amsterdam).
Originally published in BWSA 2 (1987), p. 95-97.
https://socialhistory.org/bwsa/biografie/muysken.

Photo of Kimmy Sophia Brown, Botanical Gardens, by the author

Photo of Carl Falkenberg Brown, photographer unknown

Photo of Norman Brown and Baroness Helen Dean Falkenberg Brown,
photographer unknown

Painting of Baron Gabriel Henriksson Falkenberg of Trystorp, Sweden
Oil on canvas, 144x114 cm, by Lorens Pasch the Elder. Date unknown. Cropped.

Painting of Countess Beata Margareta Douglas, oil on canvas, 78x64 cm.
by Lorens Pasch the Elder. Date unknown. Painting is cropped.

Painting of Cunradt von Falkenberg. Oil on canvas, 192x105 cm.
by Jacob Heinrich Elbfas. Date unknown. Painting is cropped.

Photo (cropped) of Baron Gerhard Knut Alfrid Falkenberg, by Johannes Jaeger.

Painting of Falkenberg of Trystorp Coat of Arms, by Jan Raneke, 1982

Photo of Jonathan Brown, photographer unknown

Painting of William Wentworth Brown
by Frederick Porter Vinton, Boston, MA, USA
Painted in 1902, oil on canvas, 4' x 5' (framed), commissioned for $1,600.
Used with permission of the Brown Memorial Library, Clinton, ME.

Photos of family at Vaughan Street, Portland, ME, photographer unknown

Photo of author on bicycle at Vaughan Street, Portland, ME, by family member

Photo of author at Crescent Beach, Cape Elizabeth ME, by James Brown

Photo of author at Two Lights, Cape Elizabeth, ME, by Kimmy Sophia Brown